Descend to Darkness

Also From Heather Graham

Aura of Night
Voice of Fear

Night of the Blackbirds
Never Sleep with Strangers
Eyes of Fire
Slow Burn
Night Heat
Danger in Numbers
Crimson Summer

From 1001 Dark Nights
Blood Night
Hallow Be The Haunt
Crimson Twilight
When Irish Eyes Are Haunting
All Hallow's Eve
Blood on the Bayou
Haunted Be the Holidays
The Dead Heat of Summer
Haunted House
Blood Night
Hallow Be the Haunt

Descend to Darkness

A Krewe of Hunters Novella

By Heather Graham

1001 DARK NIGHTS
PRESS

Descend to Darkness
A Krewe of Hunters Novella
Copyright 2022 Heather Graham Pozzessere

ISBN: 978-1-970077-95-7

Foreword: Copyright 2014 M. J. Rose

Published by 1001 Dark Nights Press, an imprint of Evil Eye Concepts, Incorporated

Acknowledgments from the Author

For Debbie Richardson, Teresa Davant, and Connie Perry, with tons of love and thanks.

One Thousand and One Dark Nights

Once upon a time, in the future…

*I was a student fascinated with stories and learning.
I studied philosophy, poetry, history, the occult, and
the art and science of love and magic. I had a vast
library at my father's home and collected thousands
of volumes of fantastic tales.*

*I learned all about ancient races and bygone
times. About myths and legends and dreams of all
people through the millennium. And the more I read
the stronger my imagination grew until I discovered
that I was able to travel into the stories… to actually
become part of them.*

*I wish I could say that I listened to my teacher
and respected my gift, as I ought to have. If I had, I
would not be telling you this tale now.
But I was foolhardy and confused, showing off
with bravery.*

*One afternoon, curious about the myth of the
Arabian Nights, I traveled back to ancient Persia to
see for myself if it was true that every day Shahryar
(Persian: شهريار, "king") married a new virgin, and then
sent yesterday's wife to be beheaded. It was written
and I had read that by the time he met Scheherazade,
the vizier's daughter, he'd killed one thousand
women.*

*Something went wrong with my efforts. I arrived
in the midst of the story and somehow exchanged
places with Scheherazade — a phenomena that had
never occurred before and that still to this day, I
cannot explain.*

*Now I am trapped in that ancient past. I have
taken on Scheherazade's life and the only way I can
protect myself and stay alive is to do what she did to
protect herself and stay alive.*

*Every night the King calls for me and listens as I spin tales.
And when the evening ends and dawn breaks, I stop at a
point that leaves him breathless and yearning for more.
And so the King spares my life for one more day, so that
he might hear the rest of my dark tale.*

*As soon as I finish a story... I begin a new
one... like the one that you, dear reader, have before
you now.*

Prologue

The night before Halloween

Oddly, it was the silence that Angela Hawkins first noted as she slowly came to—having absolutely no idea where she was.

And worse.

She had no clue how she had gotten there.

There was always sound as she woke. The covers whispering if Jackson had risen before her. One of the kids shrieking or laughing from their room. A bird trilling from a tree, or even the rustling of the branches outside their window.

But this...

It was so silent, the lack of noise seemed louder than the most horrific scream.

When she opened her eyes, she saw what she expected...

Nothing. Nothing because of the complete and total darkness.

She lay still for a few seconds. Then she reached out. There was nothing beside her, nothing above her. And below her... stone. Icy-cold stone.

She fought the sense of panic rising within her. She had to think back. She needed to remember where she had been, what had been happening.

And how in God's name she had come to be wherever she was.

Chapter 1

The sun was already lowering, the dying shades of gold and mauve in the sky touching the Gordon Town Cemetery as if with great reverence, creating soft crimson blushes on tombstones and aging mausoleums. The breeze in the air warned that winter was coming and held just a touch of chill. In minutes, the sun would drop farther, and eerie shades of gray and shadow would creep over the place, enhancing all that was ancient and decaying. While still in use, the cemetery was indeed old—and, naturally, deemed haunted.

And while it might well be, Angela Hawkins Crow knew it was the living who were deadly.

It was the week of Halloween.

Once upon a time, it had been one of Angela's favorite times of the year. Dress-up was fun. And with kids, trick-or-treating was great—even haunted houses could be entertaining.

And all that could still be true.

But, sadly, something about the holiday seemed to draw out the scaries—and not the fun kind. The lethal ones.

Such as here.

The cemetery wasn't highly visited, though it was on the national register. Visitors to the DC and Virginia areas generally came to visit Arlington and pay their respects to those who had fought for the country. They even went to Hollywood Cemetery in Richmond, where many from the Civil War had been laid to rest.

Gordon Town Cemetery was comparatively small, and many stones and markers had been lost through the years. Old mausoleums decayed as the growth of tree roots, and the simple fact that nature had taken over, chipped and broke the stones.

But as the sun fell, the cemetery was one of the most atmospheric to be found. Its lichen and ivy-covered stones, moss-covered oaks, and beautiful statuary were enchanting. Here, stone angels knelt in prayer, cherubs wept over children's graves, and intricately carved crosses rose here and there. Personal adornments marked other sites, such as the carved dogs who gave comparatively new reverence to a woman who had spent her life saving rescue animals. There were no *old* and *new* sections. Families in the area owned small mausoleums or tombs or spaces in family plots.

While it wasn't as popular a destination as many other graveyards or cemeteries, it did become well visited during the holidays—especially Halloween.

At Thanksgiving, the living descendants of those buried at Gordon Town decorated with fall leaves, plush turkeys, and other such traditional items. At Easter, they used baskets of colored eggs and bunny rabbits. At Christmas, the place was beautiful. Those who remembered the dead brought all manner of ornaments and even Nativity scenes. Flowers showed up now and then, but in an article written about the cemetery that mentioned Benjamin Robertson, a descendant of the Revolutionary hero Ethan Robertson, it said the decorating done by many of those with loved ones or antecedents was because they preferred the concept of sharing holidays to the tradition of bringing flowers. Benjamin Robertson had recently lost his father, now interred in the family crypt, and his dad had loved everything spooky at Halloween. So...

People decorated the graveyard for the October holiday. No matter how bizarre it might seem, dangling skeletons and witches on broomsticks were scattered here and there throughout the burial ground.

Gordon Town was an active cemetery.

And so it was that the freshly dug land in the center of a society plot or an extra body in a mausoleum might go unnoticed. But a young woman had come to pay homage to her father that afternoon, bringing a Frankenstein's monster doll and a stuffed ghost to set upon his grave, only to see a dark figure brandishing a knife—one she could have sworn was covered with blood. The local police had thought her hysterical or a victim of a Halloween prank since the cemetery had been done up to the nines for the holiday. But Cassandra Valois, one of the managers at the cemetery office, had heard about the so-called prank. And since her father was one of Adam Harrison's closest friends, she'd called the

Krewe's assistant director. Adam had called Jackson, and...

Here they were. They weren't alone in the cemetery as darkness fell. Colleen Law, with fellow special agent and spouse, Mark Gallagher, had also arrived, along with Special Agents Kat and Will Chan.

The cemetery was laid out in a triangular shape that cut into the Virginia woods, and they had agreed to start separately at the three angles and meet in the middle.

The place was something of a stone jungle from the get-go. Family and society crypts or mausoleums were mixed with single, aboveground tombs, stone headstones, and flat markers. The growth of trees and brush between all provided ample opportunity for shadows and mysteries—along with the many Halloween decorations now *haunting* the place.

Angela glanced over at Jackson. He hunched, studying the dirt of a family plot. While there was still light in the sky, Angela looked across the distance. An especially fine family mausoleum stood before them, probably right where they would meet up.

She started walking toward it, noting the name *Robertson* carved deeply into the stone over the archway that rose above the metal double doors.

Things hung on either side of the massive entrance. She walked forward to get a better view of the place, shaking her head.

The decorations were ghouls: skeletons with folded hands clad in long, brown robes with hoods and attached to hooks on the mausoleum walls—probably intended to hold flowers.

"My God!"

Angela jumped. She hadn't realized that Jackson had come to stand behind her.

"Okay, we both talk to ghosts," he reminded her, smiling.

"Right. And I haven't seen any here."

"Probably too bizarre for the dead," Jackson suggested.

"Possibly. I mean... I think decorating for holidays to remember those we have lost and who are still family is great. Still..."

"Halloween," Jackson said. "Have you ever seen anything like this before?"

"I was in Savannah once, and we went to see Bonaventure. It's a truly beautiful cemetery. It was Christmas, and many of the stones and tombs had been decorated with ornaments, stars—pretty things," Angela said.

"I think the decorating thing is okay. Kind of like the Day of the Dead, but..."

"Halloween is a favorite holiday for lots of people, and it's the spooky fun that makes it so," Angela murmured. "Some of this, though."

"Seems to be the wrong side of... I don't know." Jackson shrugged. "But, hey, I have no family here. Who am I to judge, hm?" he murmured.

Angela laughed softly. "As you tell me, we are all entitled to our opinions, so long as we don't attempt to force them on others. So, I'll say it. It's creepy." She frowned suddenly, noting that the great metal doors to the mausoleum weren't locked—they weren't even fully closed.

"Jackson?" she called.

"Ahead of you," he said and was already moving forward.

She wasn't sure why she felt the way she did. She had worked in law enforcement in one way or another her entire adult life. She was a capable agent and armed, and she was an expert with her Glock.

But she was glad Jackson was with her. Of course, she loved her husband. More, she respected him as an agent and as a human being. Even more than that, though, she couldn't imagine anyone she'd rather have at her back. It was an extraordinary situation with the Krewe of Hunters. Agents often wound up with other agents as their spouses and partners, which the bureau didn't accept in most situations. But the Krewe, under Adam's assistant directorship with Jackson as the supervising field agent, was a different creature altogether. Their *gifts*—or curses—were strange and difficult to share since only a percentage of the population was born with such strange abilities.

No one ever said publicly—or even privately to others who weren't in on the minuscule spectrum of those born with the ability to speak with the dead—that the deceased helped with their cases.

They'd be laughed out of usefulness.

And Jackson was also determined that such things never be twisted to injure truth and justice. Half Indigenous, he was a passionate student of history. With the early witch trials, the dead had been helpful. And Jackson was extremely appreciative that they still were to this day.

But they could not testify in court. That was reserved for the living and restricted to good investigative work—how to prove beyond a reasonable doubt that a criminal was guilty.

The Krewe members were law enforcement; they were not judge

and jury.

"Wait up!" Angela called. Jackson was tall, an imposing man and striking with the ink-dark hair of his father's people and his mother's deep blue eyes. He could also move like the wind.

Angela was shorter and slimmer, but fast as a whip herself when she chose to be. She almost crashed into his back as they reached the doors.

Her phone rang before Jackson had a chance to grasp the brass handles and pull open the giant, carved metal door.

"Hang on. It's Kat," she said, answering the call.

Kat and Will were among the original six members of the Krewe of Hunters. Before joining, Kat had been a medical examiner. She was still their on-call person when they encountered mysteries concerning a death.

"This is absurd!" Kat said. "Will and I have been all over this place. I've seen ghosts, ghouls, witches, bats, black cats, werewolves, slasher demons, you name it. Still, we dug a bit where we noticed some disturbed earth. Referring to the map we were given, all those plots received recent burials. We checked mausoleums and crypts, and all were securely locked. Which may not mean anything. Still, I hate to say it, but I might have to agree with the local police on this one. The young lady so sure she saw a murderer might have been the victim of a prank—or her imagination. I just spoke with Colleen and Mark. They are turning up nothing. Anything your way?"

"Not sure," Angela told her. "We're at the Robertson mausoleum. You must be near us. We're almost dead-center of the triangle. The doors here weren't locked. We were about to go in to check and see—"

Angela broke off. Jackson had thrown open the double metal doors, which allowed her to see within the crypt.

The odor that emerged from the tomb was the first warning.

Daylight was truly dying. Shades of the coming night—weakening golds, mauves, and grays—fell over the contents of the crypt.

One fine mahogany coffin was in the center on a dais. Bronze lettering honored Ethan Robertson, the Revolutionary hero for whom the crypt had first been constructed. One of the two coffins set just off-center commemorated the most recent death, that of the man's descendant, Joseph Robertson.

Catacomb-like shelves on either side of the room contained countless bodies—some in coffins, others in shrouds.

The natural contents of a tomb built over two hundred years ago.

But three scarecrow-like figures hung from the catacomb shelving to the right of the tomb. Figures strung up with heavy wire, all with jackets stuffed with straw and wearing strange hats.

But faces peered out from beneath the head coverings.

Features on bodies in various stages of decomposition.

Fresh corpses that were real—one with open eyes that seemed to stare at Angela with tearful and desperate appeal.

Too late.

As the scent of death and rot continued to assail her, Angela knew the scarecrows in the tomb were anything but Halloween decorations.

"Angela. Angela, are you there?" Kat's voice came to her over the phone.

"I'm here," she whispered but then took a breath and found her voice. "And we need you here, too. Along with your medical expertise."

"Um... it's a cemetery."

"No, Kat. We've got some *newly* dead."

* * * *

Kat was one of the best medical examiners Jackson had ever known, and she now used her knowledge as an agent of the Krewe. She was the only member of their number who had first been a medical examiner. While Philip Law also had a medical degree, his was in psychiatry. His knowledge of the human mind, along with his extra talents, often helped in dealing with the criminal element.

But even with Kat at the cemetery to give them her best preliminary findings, Jackson immediately called in the city and county law enforcement and then briefed Adam.

Night fell as FBI forensic teams arrived, along with a second and third medical examiner. As they turned the site over to those with the forensic skills, Jackson and Angela headed into headquarters. It was time for his wife to perform her research magic. Kat naturally stayed behind, and Will, Mark, and Colleen would also stay until the forensic teams had finished for the evening.

"In Kat's estimation, John Doe number one has been in the tomb for approximately three months. Jane Doe has been there one month, and John Doe two was most likely killed last night. Kat believes the cause of death was exsanguination, while the method was a knife," Angela said. "No ID on the victims, and no clothing to trace. The corpses were wearing strange scarecrow costumes."

"When was the last interment in the mausoleum?" Jackson asked. "I know about the article in which Benjamin Robertson talked about decorating the cemetery for the holidays, but I don't recall seeing the exact date that his father was interred."

Angela looked up from her computer. "He was laid to rest about the same time our first John Doe is presumed to be killed and set up in the tomb. Which makes his son and now owner of the vault, Benjamin Robertson, a suspect. Then again, is it too obvious? Unless he *wanted* to be caught."

"Someone wanted them found. The vault wasn't locked," Jackson noted.

"And if it was Benjamin..." Angela murmured. "I mean, could you forget to lock a vault after slicing up a human being and leaving him or her within? Was it locked before? We have three victims, killed at three different times. If it was Benjamin Robertson, then... what? He *wanted* to be discovered? Or he loved the display. Whoever did it, the spectacle mattered."

Jackson shrugged. "Naturally, the man who owns the vault is a person of interest. Keys to the family vaults are in the family's hands. Except the cemetery keeps a copy of each key for vandalism purposes, storm damage, or other forces of nature that can cause problems. Some of the family vaults are old, and the families have moved on to other states—though they maintain ownership. So, it's more than possible that a key might have been taken and copied and even returned."

He continued. "They do have security cameras at the front office. They don't really cover anything inside except who comes and goes, but if a key was taken and copied, we can at least see who has been in the building over the last three months."

He walked over to the board that Angela had created, looking at all the dates. At this time, and even after full autopsies, they wouldn't know the exact times of death for the first John Doe and Jane Doe. Identification on the dead would help with the timeline. But even then, simply going by the date they disappeared might not be accurate. Some killers held on to their victims until they were ready to commit their final crime.

"There is little else we can do until tomorrow," Jackson said. "The local police will keep the cemetery closed. Luckily, no burials or interments are scheduled for the week. I've informed Cassandra in the cemetery office that Debbie Nolan, the young woman who witnessed the character with the knife, wasn't seeing things. She probably did see a killer. We'll need to interview all the managers and groundskeepers in the morning. We'll need to bring Debbie in, too."

"Jackson, do you think the killer saw her?" Angela asked worriedly. "If he's involved with the cemetery, he'll likely know the bodies were discovered. That could put her in danger."

He nodded. "Already thought of that. We have a patrol car watching her home."

Angela smiled at him and nodded grimly. He walked over to her and placed his hands on her shoulders. It was amazing to work with his wife. They'd met when Adam Harrison had first formed the Krewe of Hunters to investigate a case in New Orleans. And Jackson had been thankful every day since.

"Tomorrow is going to come early. And it's already late." He slipped his hands down and squeezed her biceps gently.

"At least the kids will be sleeping." Angela placed her hand over his.

He smiled, thinking of Mary Tiger at home watching the kids. "Let's hope."

"Except I feel bad. They are so excited about Halloween. I'm sure Mary has seen a half-dozen possibilities for their costumes. Corby is imaginative and helps Victoria become more and more so, too. I think she would have been happy being Spider Baby, but Corby likes to get a bit ghoulish."

He chuckled his agreement.

"Ghoulish. Just what we need," Angela said. She gave a little shudder and made a face. "We have to find whoever did this, Jackson."

"We will. It's what we do," he reminded her gently.

She stood suddenly. "Right. We're on it in the morning. But now... a shower. I feel that I still smell like death," she finished quietly.

He wrapped his arm around her and started them toward the door. "Then let's go."

They did. At home, they found that the children were indeed sleeping. Mary, Axel Tiger's aunt, was the best caretaker in the world, and they knew they were incredibly lucky to have her. She said that she was lucky to have them.

Mary was watching television when they came in but quickly greeted them. She frowned a bit with worry and asked about the case, then told them, "Well, I took pictures tonight as Corby dressed himself up—and enhanced a few of Victoria's ideas. But I think I'll show them to you later. I'd best be getting home, and you should get some sleep."

Angela, of course, still wanted to see the pictures.

As expected, Corby, nearly a teenager now, had come up with all kinds of bizarre costumes. A few were just fun, from a member of the old rock band KISS to a Marvel superhero, a demon, a dark angel, and a ghoul.

They managed to smile through the pictures.

Then Mary was gone. Angela looked at Jackson and grinned, blue eyes shining like sapphires.

"Race you!" she said.

"Race me?"

"Shower."

He let her beat him, though they both had to slow down to secure their service weapons, always carefully locked in the mini-vaults by the bed because of the children.

But their clothing still wound up strewn everywhere, and they burst into the shower together, laughing, with Jackson warning her they might not get anywhere if they tripped one another or fell because of the slickness of the tile.

Slicker still when the soap came out, both of them washing themselves and then each other, the determination for absolute cleanliness their one concession to the night they had just passed. They had learned long ago that to do what they did, they had leave work behind when they came home. That afforded them sanity and a real life with Corby and Victoria.

And themselves.

They should have been tired. They *were* tired. But soaping and shampooing each other became something erotic, slick hands sliding here and there, bodies pressing. Fingers touching and caressing...

It was Angela who laughed softly and whispered that it wouldn't be terribly sensual or exciting if one of them broke a leg attempting something romantic in the shower.

Jackson had to be a little romantic, though. So, he swept her up to step out of the stall, then held her close and headed out of the bathroom. Angela grabbed for towels and assured him that he was incredibly romantic but it wouldn't lend itself to a great night if they totally soaked the bed.

"Oh, you romance-crusher," he accused her.

"I'll make it up to you," she promised.

She did. He smiled, gazing into her blue eyes, and felt the slide of her body against his. Her touch, her caress. Her kiss.

Again, he had a moment when he thought about how incredibly lucky he was. She was practically a super-agent at work. And at home?

She could make all the ugly and cruel in the world go away.

Making love expended the last of their energy. Angela whispered that she loved him, and even as he replied, he realized that she was asleep, curled against his shoulder.

He held her.

Then he closed his eyes and slept, hoping that neither of them contemplated the horrors of what they'd found in the tomb in their dreams.

Chapter 2

Two days before Halloween

"Debbie, I know how upsetting this must be for you," Angela began, speaking with Debbie Nolan, the young woman who had reported the man with the bloody knife at the cemetery. "But—"

"No one believed me," Debbie said miserably. "Of course, they do now. But I was terrified. There was a minute, or at least a second, when I thought he turned and might have seen me. But one of the caretakers was on a cart going down the path, and he wasn't that far past me. So maybe he didn't see me. I was afraid he would come after me if he did. Because he was real! I mean, really real. He wasn't a Halloween decoration or someone playing a prank. I saw him!"

The young woman was in her mid-twenties, small and slim with enormous brown eyes and a nervous manner. Angela reached a hand across the distance that separated their chairs in the conference room and set it gently on Debbie's knee.

"Debbie, yes. Of course, we believe you. And we need your help."

"Right. I saw the news. You found more than one body. You found three. I mean, it's a cemetery, but—"

"Yes, and I'm afraid someone was murdered recently. Any help you might be able to give us—"

"I don't know how I can help," she interrupted.

"First, tell me what he looked like."

"A monster."

"Okay, so..."

"Maybe a demon. He was wearing a Halloween costume: like a

black jumpsuit with a hood and a skeleton's mask beneath it. I know the police believed it was a prank, but there was something about him. I knew... I guess, well, people decorate. And they *do* come in costume, but usually only on Halloween day or evening."

"Okay, how tall do you think he was?"

Debbie shook her head. "Regular-guy size? I'm pretty sure it was a guy. I think maybe six feet and medium build?"

Angela nodded. "And where exactly did you see him? Was he headed for one of the exits?"

Debbie almost smiled. "Exits? You don't need an exit for that place. The stone wall that surrounds it isn't more than two feet high. But he seemed to be heading toward the... um, north side. Where the forest has kind of encroached on some of the stones. There's a tree that's half in the cemetery and half out. I think he ran past it and into the woods."

Angela mentally drew a map of the cemetery in her mind. Since the Robertson family vault or mausoleum was in the center of the place, he might have quickly come from it while Debbie was kneeling at her father's grave. And when she looked up, he could have easily been halfway out of the place.

"I just knew he'd killed someone. But then he was gone. And I—I didn't see anyone who had been stabbed or was bloody or... anything. And I was terrified. So, I ran. I got into my car and drove around to the office. And that lady, that Ms. Valois? She was so nice. She called the police right away, and they walked through the cemetery. But the one officer just seemed entirely disgusted by how the relatives of those buried or interred there decorate for the holiday. Some people think it's horrible and disrespectful. It really isn't. It's remembering those we love during the holidays. As if they are still with us."

"It's okay, Debbie. People remember their loved ones in different ways."

"I'm not usually scared. Most horror movies are funny to me and I like haunted houses. But I was terrified last night. So scared that when an officer called to say he'd be watching over me, I almost didn't dare believe him. I called the precinct first... and they said that I was being watched. I knew someone had found something. But even with a cop outside, I couldn't sleep. I... I loved my dad so much, but I don't think I can ever go back there again."

Angela nodded and suggested softly, "Maybe not at Halloween. And until we find out what happened, there will be an officer or an agent looking out for you."

"Thank you," she whispered. "Thank you. I—I called in sick today. I teach art at a local community college. I was so tired and scared. Then Special Agent Crow called me, but before the officer brought me here, I saw the news. I saw that three people were found in the cemetery, victims of a murderer. The blood on that knife was real."

She let out a breath. "Honestly, I'm not a horrible coward. I live by myself now in my folks' old home. My mom died when I was little. I don't even remember her. I just lost my dad two years ago, and I'm an only child. I have an alarm, but it's only on the front door. It isn't attached to any of the windows. I mean, I'm not an idiot, they're all shut and locked, but—"

"It's all right." Angela appreciated the fact that Debbie was scared and rambling. Her job was to calm her down and see if she could gather any useful information. "We know you're frightened. But no one knows if he saw you. Though perhaps you'll feel a little better if I tell you this. He knows you can't identify him. He was wearing that mask. So, he has no reason to come after you."

"What if he's just insane? He has to be a little, right?"

"I like to believe that any human being who can hurt another in that way has to be a bit off," Angela told her. "But we will protect you. An officer will be near at all times, I promise."

Debbie still looked uneasy. "Could he—or she—just come in and watch television? Then I wouldn't be so scared about the windows, especially those in back."

"I think we can arrange that," a masculine voice said.

Jackson had slipped into the conference room. He gave Debbie an encouraging smile. "And we'll set up an *assurance* program. A way for you to talk to headquarters and know for sure that a patrolman or woman is who they say they are when the shifts change. You good with that?"

"I'm grateful for that," Debbie said. "I'm so tired. I am just so, so tired."

"Officer Whittaker can take you home. Shift will change before dark, and then you'll be all set. It's going to be okay, Debbie. If you hadn't had the courage to report what you saw and insisted that it was real, we wouldn't have known anything was wrong. We wouldn't know about this killer. So, thank you. And please believe we'll look after you. That's a promise."

"Thank you," Debbie said again. Angela rose, and the young woman stood, too, looking from her to Jackson.

"It's okay. Keep our numbers on speed dial and call for anything," Angela told her.

Jackson escorted her out to the main reception area where Officer Owen Whittaker waited. He was a ten-year veteran with the force and someone his colleagues and the Krewe trusted implicitly. Angela remained in the conference room, anxious for Jackson to return.

He walked back in and frowned, likely at the look on her face.

"We have to go back," she told him.

"Back?"

"To the cemetery. Jackson, I don't know why, but... maybe we missed something. I know the forensic crews were there all night, and I know the medical examiners are still identifying the victims, but I just feel like we need to go back."

"All right. But we have several people to interview—"

"And a roster of agents ready to work," she reminded him.

"Okay. But there's someone we need to see first. One more person."

"Who?" she asked him.

He smiled grimly. "I'll bring him in."

Jackson left for a minute again and returned with a man who was speaking even as they entered the conference room.

"Horrible! Beyond horrible. What kind of a sick person would do something like that?"

Without an introduction, she knew it was Benjamin Robertson.

"Horrible. Horrible! The worst dishonor to the dead. Murder? In the tomb of a true American patriot no less. Unknown bodies left, families now feeling lost and full of fear and worry. Horrible!"

Either the man was a good actor—it was always possible—or he was truly distraught over what had been discovered in his family's tomb.

"We all agree it was terrible," Jackson said. "We're hoping you can help us."

"Me? How?"

"Nothing unusual happened when your father was interred?" Angela asked, keeping her questions polite and her manner that of someone seeking help rather than accusatory in any way.

Angela had done her research and knew the man was in his early forties. Naturally proud of his heritage, he'd written several books on the Founding Fathers. When he wasn't writing, he ran a tech company that specialized in helping those who did their own income taxes. He'd created the company along with a college buddy from Yale. The two continued to do well—so well, in fact, their employees now handled the day-to-day.

Which left Benjamin Robertson time to pursue his research and whatever other interests he might have.

Murder?

He was a handsome man with strong bone structure, curly, dark hair, and a clean-shaven face. He wasn't quite six feet tall but had a fit body for his medium build.

He wore a crisp, clean, dark blue business suit.

He frowned, looking from Jackson to Angela. "When we interred my dad? No, nothing unusual. There were no bodies in the tomb then. I mean, none that didn't belong there. Oh, my God. Even talking about this is ridiculous. Don't take that wrong. It's horrible and tragic, but..." He paused, lifting his hands helplessly. "Nothing was unusual the day my dad was interred. My pops died of natural causes—a bad heart. We knew he was also going into kidney failure, and those who knew and loved him were prepared. Ready to see him at peace. Many people attended his funeral, and the priest was in the tomb with him, too. Honestly, no, there was nothing."

"Is that the last time you were in the crypt?" Jackson asked him.

Benjamin Robertson nodded. "Other people were in there that day. Not just to honor my father, but... my several-times great-grandfather was a famed patriot. People like to see the tomb. Even architecturally, it's a historical monument."

"But you didn't leave anyone in it after the funeral?" Angela asked.

He shook his head. "No. No, of course not."

He didn't sound entirely convincing.

"And you locked it when you left. Are you certain?" Jackson asked him.

"I, yes. I'm sure. I..."

He appeared somewhat perplexed, then suddenly exploded with confusion and anger.

"I don't know! I think I locked it. I was ready and prepared for my dad's death, but it was still... it was a damned hard day. I think I locked it, but I was trying to watch over my mother and talking to the priest. To others. I think everyone was out. I think I locked it. And I probably did.

You know the cemetery office keeps a copy of the key, too."

"We do," Angela assured him quietly. "And we know how upsetting this must be for you. I'm sorry to put you through it. We're trying to get to the truth, make sure someone is held accountable, and ensure such horror never takes place again."

Robertson let out a long sigh. "Yeah, of course. I'm sorry. I guess... well, the media has it out there that bodies were found in, as they called it, the patriot's tomb. And then they act all sanctimonious, like they aren't going to say anything. The victims' families need to be notified. And, of course, they are all aware it's an active investigation. That fellow who wrote the article, Jefferson Moore, is after me again. At first, it was just fine and cool, but not now. People always want to be sensational. You know, whoever shocks the world the most gets the best ratings or reviews."

"Don't worry," Jackson told him. "It is an active investigation, and the media will not be getting anything else until we know more. But we'll speak with the fellow who did the article."

"Jefferson Moore," Robertson repeated. "I thought it was great that he wanted to write about Gordon Town Cemetery. It's notable, but it's too close to Arlington and other historic cemeteries and places that are all major sites for historians. I was glad for the opportunity to explain that decorating was a way to include our lost loved ones in our holidays. And he did a damned good job with the article. But I just don't want to talk to anyone now."

"Understandable," Jackson told him, handing him a card. "If anyone causes you difficulty, or if you think of anything, please call us."

"Absolutely," he assured.

"By the way, do you have a list of people who attended your father's funeral?" Jackson asked.

"A list? Well, it was in the paper, so..."

"Was anyone filming? Doing video?" Angela asked.

"I... I don't know," Robertson said. "Maybe. I can ask around. My cousins were there. The service was beautiful. A soprano from the church sang *Ave Maria,* and my cousin's son did an amazing job with *Danny Boy.* You never know. I guess maybe..."

"Please find out for us," Angela implored.

"My friends, my family... no one would do anything so horrible."

"But as you said," Jackson reminded him, "the funeral was listed in the paper, and you don't know who might have been there. We'll appreciate anything that might help."

Robertson offered them a grimace and said dryly, "You know, I've heard rumors. You guys are supposed to be ghost hunters or something. Maybe the dead guy can just tell you who killed him, huh?"

"That would be nice, wouldn't it?" Jackson asked, smiling ruefully. "Afraid we'll just have to do a real investigation and see what we discover. Amazing what the living can tell us when we have brilliant psychologists and psychiatrists on hand."

Robertson frowned. "You don't need a psychiatrist for this. A sick mind is sure as hell involved."

"Absolutely," Jackson agreed. "Please call us if you think of anything."

"Yes, I will. Um, am I free to go?"

"Of course. You've always been free to go," Jackson said pleasantly. "We're just seeking any help we can get."

Robertson nodded. "All right, then. You'll keep me informed on what's going on?"

"Naturally. And thank you for coming in," Angela said.

He nodded, and then Jackson told him, "I'll see you out."

Angela followed but hurried to her office and computer. She quickly did a search on the recent funeral at the Robertson tomb.

Videos had been posted to various media outlets. She wasn't sure how Benjamin Robertson could have missed the number of people who had been filming.

Most of the videos were of the priest or the singers. Benjamin had been right, the *Ave Maria* soprano had a gorgeous voice, and Benjamin's cousin's son had a lovely tenor, his tone plaintive as he sang *Danny Boy*.

But one video also showed the tomb and the crowd surrounding the service outside what would become the deceased's final resting place.

At least twenty-five to thirty-five people attended, each who might easily be identified.

Jackson came into her office. "You found video?"

She nodded.

"I just got a call from Kat. They identified the second John Doe— our killer's latest victim."

"And?"

"His name is Arnold Kern. Until recently, he worked for Robertson Technologies."

"Benjamin Robertson's company?" Angela asked.

Jackson nodded gravely. "They let him go not that long ago. He has a record, something he kept hidden at first. But, apparently, it was information that came out when the human resources department did a deeper dive on some of their employees. He had a drug conviction. However, he didn't do any time. Was only put on probation."

Angela sat back, frowning. "That doesn't make sense. I mean, Arnold Kern was the one who lost his job. If there was going to be a murder... Well, what are the most common motives? Money, love, jealousy—or revenge. But if revenge were the case in this, wouldn't Benjamin Robertson be the one in trouble?"

"Ah, well, that's when there *is* a real motive for murder. And when it's not someone who is, in layman's terms, batshit crazy."

"But this doesn't seem random."

"No, it doesn't. Anyway, despite the state of decomposition in our other victims, Kat said they're hoping for identifications on them soon. There might be a connection between the victims. We'll have to speak with Benjamin Robertson again."

"But not now. Jackson, I really want to get back into the cemetery."

"All right. But we have video now to scan."

"Philip will be a lot better at watching the video and determining what might have been going on with someone."

Philip Law, like his sister, Colleen, was a valuable member of the Krewe. They were two of a set of triplets, and the third member of their trio, Megan, was now married to Agent Ragnar Johansen. She had kept her day job, editing for a major publishing house. Still, with her ability to read between the lines, so to speak, she often helped out.

Philip, however, had degrees in not only psychiatry but also psychology, in addition to his talent for something akin to mind reading.

Jackson nodded his agreement. "I already have him listening to the recordings I made in the conference room this morning—our sessions with Debbie Nolan and Benjamin Robertson. I'll ask him to look at the videos that were posted of the funeral, as well. Mark and Colleen can help him with that. I've also requested the security recordings from the cemetery's office. Later, we'll get it all up on the main screen and see if any of us can find anything suggesting someone might have been at the funeral or in the office absconding with a key. Plus, we still have the office personnel to interview. And so many others. Then again, Rome wasn't built in a day—"

"Jackson, we have to figure out how to build Rome in a day—or at most a couple of days."

"Because?"

"Because I'm afraid if we don't, something even worse will happen by Halloween."

He grimaced. "Okay, so we'll build Rome in day or two. Come on. We can head out for the cemetery now. Maybe, if we're lucky, we'll find someone among the dead who might be able to give us something we can't get from the living." He hesitated and then shrugged. "Maybe revenge could go the other way. But it's hard not to wonder how an employee of Robertson Technologies ended up in the Robertson tomb."

"Too obvious, perhaps? Someone who wants to see him blamed for the murder?" Angela suggested.

"That's a possible theory, yes. Anyway, let's head out and trust our fellow agents to use their talents to uncover what they can see and hear in those conversations on the videos."

Angela nodded and closed her computer. They headed out to the parking lot.

The drive to Gordon Town and the Gordon Town Cemetery took them about twenty-five minutes. While the Krewe offices were in northern Virginia, traffic getting out of the D.C. area was seldom easy.

And yet it was strange. They went from an area that was heavily populated and continually congested to roads with almost nothing.

Finally, they reached Gordon Town and the cemetery.

The place remained roped off—yellow crime scene tape stretched around the entire burial grounds from triangle point to triangle point. And the local police presence was visible as intended. Before hopping over the stone wall by the embankment where they'd parked the car, Jackson waved to an officer and produced his credentials. The officer nodded and approached.

"Anyone trying to get in?" Jackson asked.

"Not in this area," the man told him and waved a hand in the air. "No way the media missed what happened last night. Captain Denning held a press conference this morning, warning people to stay away. Not quite anything like 'trespassers will be shot,' but a serious suggestion that they might be arrested. He has a way with words. So, no problems here."

Jackson thanked him, and they slowly headed toward the Robertson tomb.

Angela linked her arm with his, looking about as they moved along.

"There!" she said suddenly.

Jackson paused, looking in the direction she'd indicated with a nod.

And there, legs folded beneath him and perched on an aboveground tomb, was a man.

One that most probably wouldn't see.

He was clad in the uniform of a Continental soldier, the basic blue coat and white shirt that George Washington had ordered in 1779. Even at a distance, Angela knew the uniform from a few of the deceased she'd made friends with throughout the years. This uniform had a red facing with white lining and white buttons, typical of those worn in Pennsylvania, Delaware, Maryland, and Virginia.

"That couldn't be... Ethan Robertson?" Jackson murmured.

"That would be too lucky," Angela said.

"Probably, but I think we are in luck," Jackson said.

"Oh? Right! If it isn't Ethan," Angela said, smiling grimly at her husband, "I think it's far more than likely he indeed knew Colonel Robertson, Virginia hero of the Revolutionary War."

Chapter 3

One of Angela's best assets, Jackson thought, was her ability to appear as if she were just a friendly, interested person. It didn't hurt that she was a naturally beautiful woman with her inquisitive, bright blue eyes and fall of long, blond hair.

Nor did it hurt that her caring was real. Of course, there was that division. They had to care. But they had to keep their emotions at a distance during many investigations.

But as they approached, the ghost watched Angela curiously, his eyes on her rather than Jackson. As he realized they could see him, he smiled through a frown, surprise evident.

"Hi, sir," Angela said. "I'm Angela Hawkins Crow, and this is my husband, Jackson. We're delighted to make your acquaintance."

For a moment, the ghost looked around as if assuring himself they were actually speaking to him.

"You are seers," the ghost said. "My dear Lord, I have not met such gifted people in... ah, well, let me see. A hundred years or so."

"Really? Oh. Well, we do exist. In truth, we have many friends and coworkers who are... seers, as you say."

"What do you call it?" the ghost asked.

"We're never sure," Angela told him with a grin. "Sometimes, people think we're gifted. Others sometimes think we're cursed, but... well, I imagine you know. We don't talk about our abilities to those without them because they—"

"They think you are mad and should be locked away," the ghost said knowingly.

Angela shrugged with a grimace. "There are just so few in the world's population who are gifted. But we try our best to let our talents work for us."

"You are police officers?" the ghost asked.

For a moment, Jackson was surprised. The first *police* force in the United States had been formed in Boston in 1838—years after this man's death, he imagined.

Apparently, the ghost read the question in his expression. "I have been here a very long time," he said softly. "And I learn all I can about the world and this country as the years go by. Shifts occur, people change, and there is always something new to learn."

"We're FBI," Jackson told him. "A special unit. As far as our official doctrine goes, we handle unique cases where people *think* a place is haunted or where criminals use demonology or the like to commit their crimes."

"Ah, well. Of course. You cover up the truth for your sanity," the ghost said knowingly. "That is fascinating and wonderful."

"We hope you can help us," Angela said softly.

The ghost offered his hand. "Colonel George Clayborn, Continental Army," he told them.

They touched air, but shaking the man's hand was proper since he'd offered the gesture. While they couldn't feel him, the air was just a little bit... different.

"Colonel," Jackson acknowledged, and Angela smiled and nodded to acknowledge the introduction.

"FBI," Clayborn said. "Yes, you see, I know about that, too. Founded July 26, 1908. The investigative force of the Department of Justice."

"Yes. You're well-informed," Angela told him.

The ghost shrugged with a grin. "I've always enjoyed reading. Even with the internet these days, people are always forgetting newspapers in the cemetery. And since television, there's an old pub down the road that carries the news most of the time. As I said, I like to keep up to date."

In a serious tone, he added, "You are obviously here now because of the murders. I assumed you were police or law enforcement because no one else is allowed in the cemetery right now."

Jackson nodded. "We were—"

"Hoping to meet someone like you," Angela finished.

Clayborn sighed. "I wish I could help you. I can tell you that the Robertson vault is famous in its way. People hear about the patriot Ethan Robertson's mausoleum being here, and some know the vault was built by a famous architect of the day, Gervais Conte. So, yes, people do come sometimes."

"Have you seen anyone going into the vault? A young woman claims she saw a figure with a knife, and the door wasn't fully closed or locked. That's how we found the victims. There were three bodies in the tomb that didn't belong there. They were killed at three different times. You never saw anything?" Jackson asked.

"I saw all manner of people when the last Robertson was interred," Clayborn said and then winced. "But I never saw anyone enter and not leave. The groundskeepers go into the vaults now and then. At this cemetery, they check structural integrity. I am afraid I don't pay much attention. It is as it has been for years and years."

"It's a pity that Ethan Robertson isn't here," Angela murmured.

"Ah, Ethan was here. He had to see the end of all we fought for. All he had died for," Clayborn said. "But one glorious day, we bid him farewell after he saw the Fathers put down freedoms in writing. When he saw that our General George was heading the country but not as a king, rather as president. So, I'm afraid it's been a while. Still..." he said and then paused, frowning. "I don't think the Robertson mausoleum was closed after the last interment. There were so many people at the funeral. Some came in honor of the dead, grieving, finding prayers and a funeral to be a step in that process. Others wanted to peek inside and see shrouds covering the bones of many of those long dead."

He looked thoughtful for a moment. "As he left that day, Benjamin Robertson seemed distracted. There was a writer fellow who came, one who wanted to interview him about the decorations that would be set out for Halloween. They were talking and, well, perhaps he forgot to lock the vault. I was there, and I don't remember him with his keys."

"That was three months ago, give or take a day?" Angela said.

The ghost nodded seriously. "I heard some of the conversation, much of what went into the article. I managed to read it when a tourist forgot a pile of her papers along with the article. She left them on old Rory's grave over there." He nodded toward another of the aboveground tombs. "People are always leaving things in cemeteries."

Angela glanced at Jackson. He knew they were both likely thinking two things: The writer of the article needed to come in, and they might find something by the tomb.

One would imagine this murderer would be careful, but...

He'd started killing at least three months ago. Until now, he'd seemingly gotten away with it. But that might mean he was getting comfortable. Possibly careless.

He couldn't have returned to the mausoleum to check once the news had gone out that his victims were discovered. The police had closed the place, and they were being vigilant.

"I can ask around," Clayborn told them. "There aren't many of us here. And as you can imagine, we spend most of our time away from here among the living, watching over our descendants. But we sometimes gather at night when nothing much else is going on. You are welcome to check back with me." He grinned. "I hang here. This is my tomb. If you're looking for me, I'll be here. *Hang.* Funny expression, but I hear it all the time."

"So they weren't saying that during the Revolution, eh?" Angela teased.

He grinned. "They were not. But every decade, every year it seems, we have new expressions. New problems. And, sadly, old problems keep reemerging. Seek me out again. It's been quite lovely to spend time with you."

"It's been our pleasure, sir," Jackson assured him. "And we thank you, sincerely."

"I am here to do what I can," he said.

Angela smiled and thanked him again, then turned and walked toward the Robertson mausoleum. Jackson joined her after nodding to Clayborn.

"He must have been an incredible man," Angela murmured.

"An amazing man, an amazing soul," Jackson said. "Of course, the dead don't naturally haunt the cemetery or graveyard where they lay. Not much sense in that. But... hopefully, he will find someone who saw something." He grinned. "While *hanging* around."

"Right," Angela said. "Oh, and technically, this started off as a graveyard. There was a church, which moved when the congregation grew too big. It's called a graveyard when there are burials around a church. Cemeteries really came into being during Victorian times. And while we refer to the family mausoleums as vaults, a vault is usually in a cliff. It's a tomb or mausoleum when it's free-standing on grounds such as these."

A smile graced his lips. "Always a font of knowledge." Arching a brow, he asked, "And?"

"Right. That doesn't help us at all." She laughed. "Just talking. And here we are."

They stopped at the entrance to the Robertson tomb. The door remained ajar, just as the crime scene units had left it.

But Jackson started walking the area in front of the heavy metal doors.

A patch of grass and a small walkway led down to the winding gravel lanes that went through the cemetery. He moved slowly, studying every tiny stone, speck of dirt, and blade of grass. Of course, he reminded himself that the area had been trampled in the time between now and when the killer had left their last victim. Forensic experts had been in the vault along with the medical examiners. But their concentration had been on the tomb and the newly dead.

Nothing, nothing, nothing...

Then, something just a little off-color in the grass and dirt caught his attention—amber rather than white or the brownish color of the dirt or the green of the grass.

He bent low, reached into his pocket for an evidence bag, and carefully extracted what he had found.

It was the butt of a cigarette.

The MEs and crime scene techs would never have been smoking at a crime scene, even if they did smoke. Of course, anyone might have been walking in front of the tomb. But it might well lead them to someone they already had on their radar.

He wanted the DNA from it.

"Angela?"

With the butt safely in the evidence bag, he stood and looked around. She was nowhere to be found. He circled the tomb again, then realized the door was further ajar.

She had gone on in. He hurriedly entered himself.

She stood by the dais and coffin where Ethan Robertson lay, a frown furrowing her brow.

"What is it?" Jackson asked.

The tomb's air held a strange stillness, and the faint scent of decay and decomposition remained, even though the recently murdered and ghoulishly displayed victims were gone and at the morgue for their autopsies.

"Did they miss anything?" Jackson asked her, wondering at her expression.

Angela shook her head. "It's not that... I mean, our people are good, and the city's people are good, too. I'm sure they went over the inside of the tomb with a fine-toothed comb, so to speak."

"Then what is it?" he asked.

She shook her head. "Something about the tomb itself is bothering me," she told him. "I have no idea what it is, but..."

Angela paused, shrugging. "Maybe it will pop into my head at three a.m. or something. But... well, I'm sure we'll be back here. I think I may study up on the architect who designed the mausoleum. You never know. Something in its history might—"

"Maybe," he told her. "Remember, we're just beginning this investigation, and answers never really come easily."

"I know. And it has been a successful day. At the very least, we have a contact now in Colonel Clayborn. A good contact."

"That is true. And I don't know if it will mean anything or not, but I found a cigarette butt just outside the entrance."

"It will be interesting if we can match it up to one of the people on our radar. Or if we see in the videos—those we found of the funeral—that no one was smoking. That would likely mean that someone was here at a different time. Again, that doesn't necessarily mean anything, but it *could* mean something. Every little detail matters," Angela said.

"I think we should head back, find out how the interviews have gone, and get the writer into headquarters."

"Right."

She remained, that strange frown knitted into her forehead.

"Angela?"

"Yep, yep."

But instead of heading out, she turned around and approached the side of the coffin in the center, moving from the door to walk around the rectangular inside of the tomb.

Jackson followed her.

In most modern mausoleums, coffins were sealed into the wall, the names and dates of birth and death recorded on the marble slabs that sealed the dead into their slots. But the Robertson tomb was very old. Coffins lay on shelves. And deteriorating shrouds covered other remains that had been reduced to little more than bones, dust, and bits of fabric. Pieces of metal were here and there, maybe a watch, a pendant, or something worn and cherished by the deceased that had been left with their remains.

"I'm thinking of New Orleans, I guess," Angela said. "You know, how remains are set in family vaults. The sun is so hot it naturally cremates a body in a year and a day. There can be horrid heat in this area, too, but they don't sweep the remains into holding cells at the end here so another body can be put in its place. I guess they were out of shelving room. Maybe that's why they created a dais for Benjamin's father next to Ethan's."

"Possibly," Jackson agreed, studying each of the shelves himself.

He didn't see anything that appeared to be anything but what it should be.

At last, Angela threw up her hands.

"Let's go. We may have to come back. Or whatever is driving me nuts might come to me later. Besides, you're right. We need to question the living."

Colonel Clayborn was not sitting on his tomb when they exited the Robertson mausoleum.

"Maybe he's seeking help from a friend," Angela murmured.

"Let's hope. We'll look for him again tomorrow. I think he was probably a fine and ethical man in his day—and he has remained behind in hopes of being useful."

"Colonel Clayborn said that many stay to watch over their families, which we knew. But I feel bad. I forgot to ask if he has family in the area," Angela said. "I noted the date of death on his tomb. He survived the Revolution and died in the early 1790s."

"He's been gone for over two hundred years," Jackson noted.

"But that doesn't mean he still doesn't have family in the area. I may do some research on him, too. After we've gotten through a lot of other questions, of course."

Jackson nodded, heading for the car. "I want to get this cigarette butt I found to the lab. You drive. I'm going to put a call through to Patrick and ask him to get someone talking to Jefferson Moore. I want to speak to the man."

"Of course."

They returned to the car, and he called Patrick. He was with Mark and Colleen and had already listened to the interviews they'd conducted that morning. Now, the three of them were watching all the videos they could find on the big screen in the third conference room.

"You're on speaker," Patrick told him. "Did you get anything?" he asked.

"So are you," Jackson said. "And, yes, we acquired a new friend."

"Ah. A dead one, I take it?"

"Colonel George Clayborn. He couldn't tell us much, but I don't think Benjamin Robertson locked the vault when he left after his father's funeral," Jackson said.

"Maybe that was it," Patrick murmured.

"That was what?"

"I told you, I listened to the tapes of the interviews you did with Benjamin Robertson and Debbie Nolan. There was just something in the way they were speaking. They weren't lying, but they weren't telling you everything they were thinking, either. I couldn't quite read *what*, though. Anyway, I think we should speak with them again. Maybe shake things up. One of us should maybe just drop in and tell them we're reporting on what we have—which right now isn't much."

"At least we know one thing. It doesn't seem the key was stolen and copied from the office, then. Not if the door has remained open for the last three months," Angela said.

"Ragnar went to the cemetery's office. And while she's not official, he took Megan with him. She read between the lines, so to speak, as they talked with the people there, and it made it easy for Ragnar to say that he wasn't accusing anyone of anything. They were just stopping by on the way to lunch, hoping that maybe someone could help."

The Law triplets—Colleen, Patrick, and Megan—each had something a little bit extra. More than just the ability to speak with the dead. Colleen could hear a whisper a mile away. Megan, who never entered law enforcement and was happy with her day job, had an uncanny ability to read between the lines of what a person was saying— just as she could read between the lines of a book.

Patrick could *read* things in the human mind, which was why he had begun his collegiate education majoring in psychology and psychiatry, using his talents with the Philadelphia Police Department before becoming entangled in a case with the Krewe. After that, he entered the academy to become a part of it.

"Thanks, Patrick. How is it going with the videos?"

"Interesting. We're making our way through. It was a beautiful service, as I guess you've seen already. The singers were damned good. But there were a ton of people there. We're going bit by bit. We'll see."

"What about the writer? The guy who did the article on the cemetery. I understand he was there."

"Yes, he was. I had to look him up online. Got a picture of the man. Young fellow, early thirties. While others were watching the singers or the priest, *he* was watching Benjamin Robertson."

"I want to get him into headquarters. We're on our way back. I'm going to run to the lab, but I'd like to talk to him soon. Apparently, he called Benjamin Robertson again after the bodies were discovered," Jackson said.

They heard a chair scrape.

"We've got an address. I'll go on over and see if he's home," Mark said. "Colleen can keep at these videos with Patrick."

"Wherever I'm most useful," Colleen murmured.

"Thanks," Jackson said.

"Colleen." Angela motioned for him to bring the phone closer. "If you guys take a break, will you start digging up information on an architect for me? The man who designed the tomb. A Gervais Conte."

"Will do," Colleen promised.

"Thanks. Jackson, my phone is ringing—"

"Got it."

She had it sitting on top of her bag as she drove.

He frowned, seeing the name on the screen.

It was Debbie Nolan. He glanced at Angela and held up the phone so she could see. She nodded with a frown, and he answered the phone quickly.

"Jackson Crow."

"Help! Oh, my God, help!" Debbie cried.

Chapter 4

Jackson had suggested to Angela that she could stay and interview Jefferson Moore, but she had said that would have to wait. She felt that she might be the calming factor for Debbie Nolan.

While they arrived as quickly as possible at the young woman's home, they weren't the first on the scene. Although he'd had some difficulty understanding Debbie on the phone since she had been so hysterical, Jackson *had* ascertained that Officer Whittaker had disappeared.

They knew Owen Whittaker. They often worked with local police on problem situations. There was no way the man would be derelict in his duty, which meant that someone had forced him to leave. But that also meant he might still be alive. If so, he was most probably in danger. Someone needed to get there fast. Jackson had seen to it that the closest police presence was called in, and they arrived on the scene almost instantly.

He and Angela met an Officer Channing as they reached the yard. The man was grim, seemed concerned, and had been searching in front of the house, thrashing through the bushes, when they arrived. But he knew them—many of the local officers knew the Krewe members.

"Miss Nolan is in the house, still tearing it apart, room to room," he told them. "My partner and I haven't been able to calm her down, but we've checked out his car. He's not in it. We even forced the trunk, but he wasn't stuffed into that either. Someone pulled the wiring on the security system. It wasn't a great one to begin with, but Miss Nolan was smart enough to have a camera covering the front at the very least. No alarm was triggered, and the door wasn't forced. Whoever came and whisked Officer Whittaker away had to be someone he knew or expected."

The man had spoken all of that in a rush. Then he winced and added, "I'm worried, Special Agent Crow. I've worked with Whittaker for years. He's as solid and ethical a man as you can get. He didn't just walk off the job."

"We know, Officer Channing. No one thinks he shirked his duties. We will get to the bottom of what happened," Angela promised. "Excuse me. I'll try to calm Debbie down and find out if she can tell us anything."

"Miss Nolan said she was in her bedroom folding clothes, felt hungry, and came out to the living room to ask if Officer Whittaker wanted something to eat. He had been on the sofa when she went to see to her laundry. She'd suggested that he watch a game on television—I guess they had talked, and she knew that he loved sports. Anyway, he wasn't there. The television was blaring, but she hadn't paid any attention to it. She looked through the house and then panicked, thinking that someone was still inside after doing something to her protector, and worried they'd be after her next."

"That must be when she called us," Jackson said. "As Angela said, we know Whittaker. He's a fine man. We need to find him pronto."

Channing nodded. "Right. Yes, thank you. We cleared the house and the yard. No one's here."

"We're going to need a crime scene unit," Jackson said.

"I'll see to Debbie," Angela said again. "If you'll excuse me. Oh, and, Officer Channing? Thank you."

He nodded, his eyes a little damp with misery. But she knew that he appreciated her words. Jackson nodded to her, too. They both knew the importance of everyone believing in the humanity of any situation.

They had to find Whittaker. That was their priority right now. He was one of theirs.

Angela went into the house.

Debbie Nolan kept a neat and pleasant home. The living room in her little townhouse had soft beige walls, an entertainment center, and a comfortable seating area with a sofa and several upholstered chairs that faced the television. Angela could imagine Owen Whittaker relaxed on the couch, watching a beloved game in comfort, close to the woman he had been sent to guard.

She walked through a large archway to the dining room and from there to the kitchen, where again, everything was nicely kept in middle-class comfort, tidiness, and appeal. Debbie was nowhere to be found—and neither was the second police officer.

"Debbie?"

A stairway led to two bedrooms on either side of the small landing. Debbie was seated on the bed, her head in her hands. The officer leaned against a bureau, looking exhausted.

He stood straight when he saw Angela and indicated to Debbie where she sat on the bed, sunk low in despair.

Angela nodded to the officer, and he fled the room as quickly as he could.

Angela sat by the woman and put an arm around her shoulders. Debbie looked up with tear-stained eyes. "They got him! I don't know how, but they got him. I was just up here... doing laundry, you know. I liked him so much. He was so nice. He didn't mind that I was scared and wanted him in the house. He was happy, watching the game, but he wasn't stupid or careless."

She sniffed. "I don't know who or how but when I didn't see him, couldn't find him, I was terrified and called you. I heard sirens almost immediately. I was so afraid someone was still here, but they must have gotten scared away and... oh, God. Dear God. I'm so scared. And I'm so scared for Officer Whittaker."

"Of course, Debbie. But we're here now, and the local officers came right away."

"It's all my fault."

"Debbie, someone doing criminal things is not your fault," Angela said firmly.

"But I asked him to come in. I had him sit down and watch TV. Maybe if I hadn't done that, he'd still be outside."

"That might not have changed anything."

"But whoever took him was in the house!" she cried.

"And they might have seen him outside. You can't torture yourself over this. None of it is your fault. There is an investigation because of you, and it will bring us to the truth—and maybe save a lot of people."

"I should have let them."

"Pardon?"

"I should have left him alone in the car and let whoever is doing this get to me. I assume I'm the one they want. That's just it. Maybe it would have been better if they'd gotten me. Officer Whittaker is married and has a five-year-old and a three-year-old."

"We will find him."

"Dead!" she cried again.

"No. If they wanted him dead, I believe they would have killed him right here and then gone for you. They're holding him. And we must find him. We know whoever is doing all this knows who you are. I'm still not sure how, but they came to this house, and they kidnapped Officer Whittaker. We need to get you to a safe house. One that can't be breached easily. One that can't be breached at all if possible. And don't worry. We'll have a team of agents with you. All right?"

"I just... wow. My job. I'll probably lose my job—"

"Better than losing your life. Don't worry. Our acting director, Adam Harrison, will speak with your employer. Pack up a few things. We need to start looking for Officer Whittaker. Pack your laptop, chargers, clothing—anything you'll need. No food. Our safe house is fully stocked. And we can also get you anything else you may need later. For right now, I only need you to hurry."

"Yes. Yes, of course!" Debbie stood, reached into her closet, and grabbed an overnight bag. She quickly began throwing articles of clothing, a few power cords, and her computer into it. Angela asked if she could help—she imagined that Debbie was usually the type to fold each garment carefully—but Debbie shook her head and promised she needed no more than a minute or two.

She was true to her word and was quickly ready.

When they reached the front of the house, Angela saw that Jackson was already moving on the search for Officer Whittaker.

Mark was there with Colleen. Ragnar, who had been partnered with Mark before Colleen came into the Krewe, was also there, along with Mark's dog, Red.

Red was amazing. He'd once served as a police dog, trained in bombs, drugs, cadavers, and missing persons. He'd also been certified as a service dog and could accompany Mark and Colleen on any endeavor. Jackson had apparently called in the group, asking for them to bring Red. The pup might well be their best chance at finding Officer Whittaker.

"Debbie, sorry. Wait for me for just a minute, and then we'll get a couple of agents to get you to the safe house."

"Please, Angela. Please. I know you have to work, but I will feel so much better if I can just get there with you. I mean, is anything or anywhere *really* safe?"

"Trust me, we were seriously worried about the safety of one of our people and had them at this safe house. It's state of the art, walled, gated, alarmed to the nines. It's safe. Please, just give me a minute."

She left Debbie waiting on the doorstep and hurried to join Jackson and the others on the sidewalk in front of the house.

She greeted Red first. They considered it important for the Krewe agents to recognize their canine assistants. Dogs didn't work for money. They worked for treats sometimes, but affection and approval were what they seemed to crave the most. Angela greeted the others with a nod, and Mark brought them all up to speed.

"There was a car parked just to the east of Debbie's townhouse here. Red followed the scent to that position. Someone put Officer Whittaker in a car, and then drove away."

"All right, we need to get a group of officers and agents moving down the block. See who might have surveillance cameras that can capture images out into the street," Jackson said. "And we'll need to get traffic cam footage from all the surrounding areas. Patrick is at headquarters."

"Before we got your call, Jackson, I brought in our article author, Jefferson Moore," Mark told them. "Megan came in to watch and listen with Patrick, and she's doing her best to keep him entertained now. Kat called, too. They have an ID on the Jane Doe found in the Robertson tomb. Mercy Cartwright. She was reported missing by her roommate approximately two months ago. Kat was able to secure dental records."

"She didn't happen to work for Robertson Technologies, did she?" Angela asked.

"No, she was a flight attendant," Colleen told her.

"So, no connection to the Robertson family. What about our first victim? Any connection to Arnold Kern, apparently the last corpse to join the recently murdered in the tomb?" Angela asked.

"None that we know of, but we're pulling phone records," Ragnar said.

"Okay, Colleen and Mark, will the two of you get Debbie Nolan to the safe house? You've been actively working this, and I'll get other agents on it. But for now—" Jackson began.

"I need to go with them to get her settled," Angela said. "But once we're good there, I'd like to get back to headquarters. I want to speak with the writer who did the article. He went to the last funeral, interviewed Benjamin Robertson, and wants to interview him again. If he isn't involved with this in any way, he may still know more than we do."

"I'll ask the cops helping me canvas the neighborhood. They can see if any of the neighbors saw anything or if they have cameras that might be helpful," Ragnar said and then nodded to Mark and Colleen.

"I've already called in for any traffic cam footage from the area," Jackson said. "It'll be at headquarters ASAP. Patrick can start reviewing it." He nodded brusquely. "All right, let's move."

Angela headed back to the front step of the house and smiled at Debbie, who still appeared nervous and anxious.

"Ready to go?" she asked.

"I've been ready," Debbie said. "I'm sorry, I'm sorry. It's just so upsetting."

"It's okay. It's understandable," Angela assured her. "Come on. We'll drive with Special Agents Mark and Colleen Gallagher. Oh, and Red."

"Red?" Debbie asked.

"He's a dog." Angela smiled. "He works with us."

"A dog as an agent?"

Angela nodded. "One of the best we have. I'm going to the safe house with you, but Mark and Colleen will stay until our next agents come on."

"You're leaving me?"

"I have to, Debbie. I'm sorry."

"I... I... I mean, I should just be grateful. I *am* grateful. I'm sorry."

"You're fine. It's all right. Come on."

Mark was in the driver's seat, Colleen next to him with Red on her lap, despite his size.

"Hey, Debbie," Colleen said. "I didn't know how you felt about dogs, so..."

"I, uh, I don't have one, but I like them," Debbie said, crawling into the back. Angela moved in beside her.

"Red can come back here," Angela said. "We have more room."

"Yeah, it's okay. We'll get to the safe house. I'm fine," Debbie assured them and started petting Red as soon as he settled between their seats.

Mark pulled out onto the street. As they drove, Colleen talked about

Red, trying to make the drive easy for Debbie and perhaps make the woman feel more comfortable with her and Mark. She explained his work, said that she'd had him registered and that he had now been used in almost every kind of situation imaginable as a law enforcement animal, as well.

Angela smiled as she listened. She and Jackson had dogs, too. Though they only told others about one of them: their living dog.

But they also had a ghost dog.

Both canines had adopted *them*, and then they had officially adopted the dogs.

If anyone snooped around their house, they had alarms, of course, but no creature or piece of equipment could be as ferocious and loyal as the dogs.

They arrived at the safe house. It was an impressive place.

Mark keyed in the combination at the gate and set his print on the mechanism, as well. That was something they had added recently. Debbie surveyed the wall, the gate, and the drive.

"Cameras are everywhere," Angela pointed out. "No one comes or goes from here without the pictures showing in our tech department. We have someone on at headquarters twenty-four-seven. Trust me, please. It's not just a safe house, it's *extremely* safe."

"I... yes. It looks great," Debbie said. "I wish..."

"Yes?"

"I wish I'd realized I'd been seen. That whoever it was had figured out who I was. I wish we'd come straight here. If we had, then Officer Whittaker would be..."

"Debbie, we all wish that right now," Angela assured her. "We will find him, trust me. We're good at what we do. And part of what we do is looking after people like you, who might be in danger. So, please know that none of this is your fault."

Debbie nodded.

Mark parked the car in the semicircular drive. "We're here," he said cheerfully. "And it's a great place, I promise."

"We had my sister stay here when she was in danger and involved with a case," Colleen said. "Megan isn't a Krewe member, she's an editor. But she... well, anyway, I think you met another of our team members, Ragnar Johansen? She's married to him now. Anyway, she, uh..."

Colleen paused awkwardly, and Angela hid a smile. She didn't want to explain that her sister saw and spoke to the dead—and had her special talent of what they called *reading between the lines.*

"She's just great, and we all love her," Angela said quickly. "So, let's show you the house."

Again, Mark keyed in the code and used his fingerprint to open the front door.

And then they were in.

Angela knew the house well, but Mark and Colleen would be staying. She decided they should do the tour of the place.

Mark pointed out that every window was attached to the alarm system, as were both doors. They told Debbie that she was welcome to check out the upstairs and choose a bedroom after they'd shown her the kitchen.

Red ran around, wagging his tail as he approved of their location and assured himself that no one was there.

Seeing that everything was going well, Angela knew that she should get moving. Debbie still looked stricken, but behind her, Colleen grimaced at Angela and mouthed, *"We'll be fine."*

"Jackson left Ragnar to get the police going on the house-to-house searches for the video surveillance," Mark said. "He should be out front any minute."

Angela nodded. "Perfect, thanks."

She headed out to the gate. She knew the code as well and keyed it in.

Then pressed her forefinger to the pad.

The gate opened. Someone changed the code weekly—or whenever the house came into or out of play with temporary guests.

She stood in front of the house for a minute, glancing at her phone. She had a message. Jackson was on his way to get her. She judged he'd arrive in a minute or two.

She wondered if she should have stayed behind the gate until he did, but she hadn't seen anything at the cemetery. Not to mention, the criminal carrying out these murders was unlikely to accost an agent in broad daylight, especially in an area where cameras were set to record every move.

Yet still...

As she stood there, she felt strange.

As if she were being watched.

The safe house was in a neighborhood of upper-middle-class

homes. The yards were decent-sized, and fences or walls surrounded most of the houses. A lot of them were fairly large, offering three to five bedrooms each and garages, and many had pools in the back.

There were no high-rises on the street. Which meant that no one could be watching her from a window in a tall building.

Then again...

There *was* a park across the street and down a bit. It had trees that stretched high toward the sky, handsome, well-kept bushes, and a playground just beyond. Moms, dads, kids, aunts, uncles, and friends ran about, see-sawing, climbing on the jungle gym, and just having fun.

It was ridiculous to think that someone had somehow followed them and was watching her from a tree.

Or a merry-go-round.

She gave herself a mental shake.

Debbie's paranoia was rubbing off on her. Of course, Debbie had a right to feel paranoid.

And then there was Officer Whittaker.

They had to find him. Truly. The man had children. He was loved and respected and...

They would find him. They'd procure footage from a traffic cam, at the least. And with any luck, they would identify the driver of the car in which he had disappeared, using facial recognition.

Still, the uneasy feeling wouldn't go away. She stared at the playground again.

Everything looked so normal.

Jackson drove up, and she jumped into the car with a smile as she looked at him.

"Any neighbors with cameras that showed the street?"

"Yep. And we have traffic cam footage, too. They're working it now. But I got a call from Megan. We have nothing to hold the writer on, and he's getting antsy. We're going to need to see what we can get from him. Now."

"Right. Of course."

Jackson knew how to drive and maneuver the streets of Northern Virginia and DC as few others did.

They were halfway back when Jackson's phone rang. He answered the call through the car speaker, and they glanced at each other as Megan's voice came through.

"Hey! I've been charming, I swear. I've talked about movies, books... articles, history. Great things to love about a book over other mediums. But he grew impatient and said he has a few meetings tonight. I don't think I can keep him much longer."

"Try. We're almost there," Jackson said. "Walk him out, keep talking—"

"Tell him how brilliant he is," Angela suggested, shrugging as Jackson glanced her way. "Sometimes, that works."

"All right. Still..."

It took another twenty minutes to reach headquarters. They hurried from the car and the parking garage to the office, just as a man was walking out, followed by Megan.

Megan was a beautiful woman with her soft red hair and fine features.

And she knew how to flirt—even while married.

She *was* being charming as she walked out toward the cars with the man.

Jefferson Moore.

He was young, as Patrick had said from seeing his face in the video from the Robertson funeral service.

Perhaps thirty-two or thirty-three. He was a tall man with sweeping dark hair, dark eyes, a deep tan, and a fit form.

He wore jeans and a casual beige leather jacket over a shirt that bore several colorful pictures of the late Elvis Presley.

Music lover?

"Ah!" Megan exclaimed. "Here they are now, Jeff. I'm so glad they made it back. You're going to love Angela. She shares your love of history, architecture, and all things old. Especially all those that lead to us in the present. Jefferson Moore, I'm delighted to introduce you to Jackson Crow, our fearless leader, and Special Agent Angela Hawkins Crow, who tends to be our great font of knowledge."

Megan had obviously been working hard to keep talking. Behind Moore's back, she made an exhausted face.

Angela smiled easily as she moved forward to shake the man's hand. Jackson did the same.

"Pleasure. I'm afraid I don't have much time," Moore told them. "The agent who brought me in led me to believe we could talk right away."

"I'm afraid life intervenes at times," Jackson said.

"You obviously love music," Angela said, pointing at his shirt.

"'Life is what happens while we're busy making plans,'" she said. "There's some argument over who first came up with the quote or exactly how it should be worded, but I hand it to John Lennon. I first heard it came from him. You have our most sincere apologies, and we beg your indulgence for just a few more minutes."

He grinned. "Sure. Another music lover. I can give you about ten."

"That would be great. Let's head back to a conference room," Jackson said. "Better than standing around in a garage."

"Ten minutes, one way or another," Moore said with a shrug.

They walked in. Megan had already fled. She'd apparently talked all she could to the man. When they had used up their ten minutes, and Jefferson Moore was gone, they could find out if Megan had gained any insights from him.

Once they were seated, Angela smiled at Jefferson. "I read your article. It was so intriguing. And while small and not as well-known as others, Gordon Town Cemetery *is* amazing. Your research, though, was wonderfully complex."

"Thanks. To be honest, I was most intrigued by the decorations. I mean, the Christmas stuff, the Easter bunnies and eggs, all that seems so nice. So much better than flowers—in my mind at least. But then I heard about the Halloween stuff. Quite honestly, it seems creepy. When I was a kid, I went to grade, middle, and high school in the area. We learned all about Ethan Robertson. The man was amazing. They sent him on all kinds of guerilla missions that he handled with ease. He almost single-handedly held back a horde of men at the beginning of the Battle of Yorktown. The idea of anything other than respectful decorations being at his resting place... well, it just seemed strange."

He shrugged and continued. "Then again, it's been over two hundred years since he died, and the tomb is now filled with other Robertsons and close friends or relations. In my article, I tried to make sure I expressed that history is something living. It teaches us what went wrong before. If we're lucky, we can use it to stop horrible things from happening again. I admit, I went to that funeral hoping to get a look inside the tomb. I'd tried to get through to Benjamin Robertson before, and his people just kept putting me off. But I was still fascinated. Wanted to see inside. Some old bones in nothing but shrouds, coffins... the passage of every decade can be seen in that tomb."

"The history *is* incredible," Angela said quietly. "And with your knowledge and fascination regarding the tomb, we're hoping you might have seen something. Or that—"

"You're not accusing me of having anything to do with the murders, are you?" Moore said, horrified.

"No, of course not," Angela assured, shaking her head as if in confusion. "No, no. We were just hoping you could maybe tell us something that might help with the investigation."

"All right," he said and leaned forward. "Yes. I can tell you something."

Chapter 5

Jackson frowned, waiting for Jefferson Moore to continue.

"Okay, thank you," Angela said. "Please, what can you tell us?"

"Something's going on there." He chuckled ruefully. "I mean, of course, you know that something was going on there—you found the bodies of murder victims in the tomb."

"Right," Jackson said. "But what did you see before the bodies were found? What do you know?"

"Know?" Moore asked, sitting back. "Well, I don't *know* anything. I should have said that. I don't know. The day I went to find Benjamin Robertson at his father's funeral... I don't know how to explain it. I just had a horrifically strange feeling. As if things were going on."

"Why is that?" Angela asked. "Was it something Robertson said to you?"

"No. Robertson was as good as I'd hoped, and it was a tough occasion for him. I knew that. But once I introduced myself, apologized for bothering him, and told him I hadn't been able to get through to him, he seemed almost happy and relieved to talk about something other than the service that day. He let me into the crypt and promised to meet me later at a local pub—which he did."

"So, what makes you think something was going on?" Angela asked.

Moore shrugged. "I know this sounds crazy, but I had a strange feeling around the tomb. Like a dark feeling. Something that made me think..."

"You thought the place was haunted?" Angela asked.

Moore shook his head. "It wasn't like a feeling of being haunted. I mean, I've never seen a ghost, but I've felt the presence of history, I guess you could say. The feeling of loss and sadness when you're standing on the battlefield at Gettysburg, that kind of thing. Well, at least *I* feel it."

"Many people do," Angela assured him.

"I'm sure this sounds crazy, but I just felt something... dark. Right." He sighed. "I mean, how much darker can you get than a battlefield? But war is one thing. Horrible, of course, and still man killing man. But in a war, few soldiers want to go out and kill and be killed. But they are fighting for their nations. Maybe violent death is violent death. But there is something especially heinous about cold-blooded murder," Moore said.

"But you didn't see anything in the tomb?" Jackson asked.

"Well, rotting Robertson dead," he told them. "But no... uh, no victims hanging or lying anywhere. No fresh kills. I still felt uncomfortable in the place. Had a strange feeling something ugly was under it all. I wasn't surprised when I heard what you'd found."

"But the first victim we found, at least according to the ME's educated estimation, arrived right at the same time—or just after—that funeral," Jackson said.

"Do places have a foreboding of what is to come?" Moore wondered aloud. "I don't know. And maybe it was silly and ridiculous. But, hey, I served my stint in the service. I've seen some ugly stuff, and I'm not easily—"

"Scared?" Angela said softly.

Moore grimaced. "I guess that is the word. Anyway, I'm sorry. Really. I don't actually *know* anything. I just had a strange feeling, and I still feel that way when I'm at the tomb. Almost as if..."

"Yes?" Jackson pressed quietly.

"Almost as if there is something I should see but don't," Moore said. He appeared to give himself a mental shake and then shuddered. "Sorry. Crazy, maybe. Or just the imaginative feelings of a writer." He checked the clock. "Now, I really must go—"

"One more quick question," Jackson said. "You got this feeling. But was there anyone at the funeral who appeared suspicious? Behaving curiously or just strangely?"

Moore winced. "Me, I guess. There were a lot of people there. Everyone approaching him, of course—Robertson, I mean. Giving him their condolences. As far as being in the crypt... well, it was just him and the priest. Everyone else stood just outside. He was kind enough to let me walk in with him when I told him that I wanted to write an article that explained what they did for others along with making sure that I noted the historical significance of the cemetery."

"And you've approached him again," Angela noted.

Moore nodded. "What was found there... well, I want to give him a chance to vindicate himself and clear his name. People assume he must be the main suspect. Is he? I guess he must be. But you don't say *suspect*, do you? Person of interest."

Jackson smiled. "Everyone associated with the Robertson tomb is a person of interest."

"Oh! Oh, me because of the article. I assure you—"

"Mr. Moore, you're not a suspect—I'll just go ahead and use that word," Jackson told him. "But we would sincerely appreciate hearing about anything else you may think of. Maybe looking back you'll remember someone who seemed especially interested in the tomb or the construction of it. Don't hesitate to contact us if you think of anything at all, even just more of those feelings you had in any particular place. And keep in mind, we may be seeking your help again at some point."

"Of course, of course. Feel free to call me anytime. But I think I am way over my ten minutes now. I really do need to go."

"That's fine," Angela said, rising.

Moore and Jackson stood, as well.

Moore made a strange face. "Hey, thank Megan for me, will you? She was trying so hard to be so perfectly fun and pleasant in order to keep me here. She was good. Really good." He grinned and shrugged. "Too bad she's married—and to an agent."

"Ah, well, I'm glad you two had a nice conversation while waiting. Thanks again," Angela said. "Come on. I'll see you out."

She grimaced, smiled at Jackson, and left with Moore. When she was gone, Patrick walked into the room.

"We've got something," he told Jackson.

"Great. What?"

"We found a connection between Jane Doe and John Doe number two," Patrick said. "Jordan got back from Boston an hour ago, came straight in, and decided she might best help down in tech, sifting through phone records. They made some discoveries. Just days before she was killed—by the ME's educated guess on timeline, anyway—

Mercy Cartwright was in touch with Arnold Kern. The team dug deeper into their past and discovered that calls between the two went back several months. What we need now, which is understandably difficult for the MEs, is an identification on our first victim."

"Right. At least we know now that those two knew each other. Any voice messages?"

"None."

"We don't have text messaging between them?"

"Ah, yes, I was getting to that. Just one. Mercy Cartwright texted Arnold Kern," Jordan said. "The message was initiated a day or so before she was killed."

"And?" Jackson asked. "What did it say?"

"Three words," Patrick said. "I want out."

Angela walked back into the room then and glanced over at Jackson.

"Bring her up to speed," Jackson told Patrick.

Patrick did.

"Okay. We now know they were into something together. And whoever our first victim was, he might well have been in on whatever Mercy wanted out of, too. We need an ID on the first person killed and left in the tomb," Angela said.

"We have people sifting through missing persons reports from all over the country. The body was in an extreme state of decomposition, strangely rotting and almost mummified at the same time. I'm afraid my medical knowledge is sadly lacking," Jackson said, glancing down at his phone. "I just got a text. Kat has been working this and thinks she can find something. Says she's gotten the body to a point where she can maybe pull a print."

"She had to re-hydrate the corpse," Patrick said.

"I say we head to the morgue. Jackson?" Angela suggested. "And then... would you go back to the cemetery with me, Patrick? Maybe..."

"I'm not great at reading the minds of the dead," Patrick said dryly.

"I know. But we made a friend—a soldier from the Revolution."

"And he never saw anything?"

"Not that he knows. But with your degrees in the medical field and experience delving into the human mind... I mean, he's dead, but his mind and soul are keen. Maybe you can help him remember something he doesn't know he knows."

"I'll head to the morgue," Jackson said. "You and Patrick get on over to the cemetery. Daylight only lasts so long."

"All right. Megan is reading through the article that Jefferson Moore wrote on the cemetery. Maybe she'll get something from between the lines. When Angela and I get back, Jordan and I can take over watching Debbie at the safe house. Computers work there, and we can keep on an information trail," Patrick told him.

Jackson nodded. "Good. We need to know how Mercy Cartwright and Arnold Kern met. Understanding their social lives could give us something and might help us."

"We'll get on every site out there," Patrick promised.

"Okay, back to the cemetery," Angela said. "Patrick..."

"Hm?"

"I'm tired. You're driving," Angela told him.

Patrick laughed. "You got it."

They all left together, heading to separate cars. Angela waved as she slid in next to Patrick. Jackson waved in return, settled into his car, and headed to the morgue.

He was greeted warmly in the austere reception area. He thought that it was kind of sad that he was known so well at the morgue. But he knew that what they did saved lives and brought justice for the dead.

He understood that the words *rest in peace* had real meaning.

The receptionist directed him to head down the hall. The first John Doe's corpse was in examination room three, and he suited up and headed inside.

Kat grinned when he arrived. "I knew you'd show up."

"I should have called to tell you I was on the way," he said and smiled at her. Kat was extraordinary. She was a petite blonde, smart as a whip, and while she maintained her medical certifications, she had excelled at the academy. She was also a crack-shot, and an excellent agent in every way.

She laughed softly. "No problem. I was expecting you.

"Oh?"

"This was tricky. It's almost as if the tomb allowed the body to decompose in two different climate zones. And while I'm not sure about this, I think John Doe number one here might have been dead a bit before being brought into the tomb. Maybe even refrigerated before he became part of the grotesque display. At any rate, I had to—"

"Hydrate the fingers," Jackson said.

"Right. Good call."

He laughed. "Patrick told me."

"Of course, he did." She smiled. "Anyway, I was just starting. You're welcome to watch."

A sheet covered John Doe's body, but his right hand rested on a small metal table by the gurney, where it lay near a strange little mechanism that apparently provided a slow return of moisture to it.

Kat carefully withdrew the appendage from the box, reached for the scalpel that lay beside it, and began a slow and meticulous removal of the skin.

"Sorry," she murmured. "I have to be careful. This is..."

"No, ignore me. Take your time."

Jackson had seen the worst of what man could do to others in many different ways. Still, there was something unsettling about the painstaking removal of the skin on a man's hand.

In short order, it was off.

The upper layer of skin separated.

"Now..." Kat murmured and then paused. "Actually, this will work better with you. Size-wise," she said.

"Oh, uh..."

"Yeah. I need you to put his skin on like a glove. You already have disposables on, naturally, so it's not as disgusting and creepy as you might think. I'll slide it on carefully and slowly—if you're all right with that."

"Kat, when have you known me *not* to do something when it was necessary?" he asked, offering her his hand.

The act of sliding the skin over his gloved hand was as painstaking and meticulous as the removal of it.

But then it was done. And Kat had ink pads out and ready on another table.

It took another twenty minutes at least, but in that time, they had a full set of prints for the man who lay on the gurney.

"Wonderful!" Kat said, seemingly both pleased and relieved. "I'll get these into every database we know of immediately. We might have an ID soon."

"Perfect. Great. We can get moving on this and see if the man had any contact with the other victims. If we can associate them..."

"Patrick kept us all informed," Kat said. "We know that Mercy and Arnold knew one another. But that text... it didn't sound as if they had a dating thing going on or anything like that. Nor did their jobs coincide.

Mercy made some real money, and I would guess that Arnold was respectfully paid, but from what we've seen so far on social media, Mercy played some high-stakes games. She was a flight attendant but apparently worked for several big-money people and corporations. She didn't work commercial flights, rather on private, very expensive luxury planes."

"Coming in and out of the country," Jackson murmured.

"What are you thinking? Drug deals?" Kat asked.

"Quite possibly. It's a theory for now. Keep at it. And thank you."

"Where are you off to?"

"The cemetery. I'm going to meet up with Angela and Patrick. And then I'm going to find out how our people have been doing on searching through the neighborhood videos and traffic cam footage. I believe Officer Whittaker is alive. And I intend to find him that way."

* * * *

Angela didn't see their Revolutionary War ghost when she and Patrick arrived. They checked in with the police and walked toward the Robertson tomb.

"I'm not sure what else you think we're going to find, Angela," Patrick said. "Our crime scene investigators were here. You know they went over the place more than once. That's one thing Jackson impresses on us all. We're a team, and we get things done and have results because we are a team. Yes, a bit of a different one, but still."

"I know. But... when that writer was in today, he didn't say much that was helpful. Except that he had the same feeling I've been having. Something is... off. I can't help but believe it has something to do with the tomb."

"What do you think it could be?"

She shook her head. "I want to know more about the architect who designed the place. Maybe that will help. I'd intended to look into it already—"

"Hard to do everything at once," Patrick said.

"I know. And this is my hang-up, I guess. I believe it's going to be important to find out if all three of the victims were together in something. Mercy texted that she wanted out, suggesting they were involved in something criminal."

"Or she didn't want to play *Dungeons and Dragons* with them anymore."

Angela made a face at Patrick. "Come on, Patrick, what do you feel?" she asked.

He stood still for a minute with his eyes closed.

"A depth of history," he said quietly. "Strange, something sad, something beautiful, peaceful, and something... I don't know. It's almost as if the air remembers all the things that have happened during the past two-hundred-plus years."

Angela nodded. "But more," she said softly and then noticed something. "Hey!"

"What?"

"I probably saw it but didn't really note it. There's a little American flag stuck into the ground there."

"There's everything everywhere here," he reminded her and began pointing in different directions. "Toy witches on brooms over there... a great big grinning Casper the friendly ghost over there. Oh, wow... slasher-movie killer over there. And, nice, someone put out a bowl of candy on that grave. But..."

He walked over to where the flag was stuck into the ground. "Probably a soldier buried here."

The grave had a rounded headstone. The marker denoted the final resting place of a Tammy Brighton, born January 20, 1920, deceased May 21, 2000. There was no indication that she'd served in the military.

"Some people are patriotic," Patrick murmured.

"But it's odd, right?"

"Yes, and no. Everything here is odd."

Angela smiled. "I don't know. It just seems... strange. I mean if there really was a creepy ghost on the tomb, I'd just think it normal—for here. Why does the flag seem out of place? It's about ten feet from the entrance to the Robertson tomb, and another ten feet to the north. There are markers here for other people in what I assume to be Tammy Brighton's family, and they are decorated for Halloween. I wonder if the flag is a... directional? Or..."

"You want to dig up the ground here," Patrick asked.

She huffed out a breath. "No. Yes. Maybe. Hey, look there." She pointed to a spot about three feet from Tammy. "It looks like a recent burial. I see a temporary marker. Harold Brighton, born November 3, 1939, deceased October 23 of this year."

"Okay, naturally, the ground remains..."

Patrick paused, looking around.

"Patrick?"

"I'm feeling something different. Something almost malevolent."

Angela started to walk over to him. He swung around to look at her.

"Get down!" he cried.

She didn't need to be told twice.

Falling flat, Angela reached the ground in time to hear the whistle of a bullet flying past.

A bullet that would have struck her dead-center in the chest if she'd still been standing.

Chapter 6

As Jackson parked on the outskirts of the cemetery, he was surprised to see a patrol car pull up and the ghost of Colonel George Clayborn slide through the door of the rear right passenger side, unnoticed by the officer who had been driving the car.

Clayborn saw Jackson and nodded, aware he needed to wait for the officer to approach Jackson before he spoke to him.

"Special Agent Crow," the officer said in greeting. "Anything more on finding Officer Whittaker?"

"I believe our experts will have something they can give us on video shortly of whoever took off with Officer Whittaker. We have a few great dogs in the Krewe, and one of our best scent dogs found a trail that let us know he was put into a car and driven away. If we can trace some of the video, we'll have an idea where to focus a search."

"Thank you. That's the hardest thing. Not knowing where to begin," the officer said. "Anyway, sorry to interrupt your work here, but... well, yeah. Everyone loves Whittaker. We're all praying he's still alive. We almost don't understand why we're still... I mean, what was discovered here was horrible, but those victims are dead. We can only pray that Whittaker is still alive. He needs to be found before he ends up like the others."

"We are well aware of that," Jackson assured him. "But if we can figure out what happened here, we can narrow down who took Whittaker."

"Yeah, right. Sorry. I, uh, sorry." He smiled awkwardly. "I didn't mean to interrupt you here, and I know you guys don't really keep hours, but it will be dark soon. The cemetery has lights, but between the density of the woods and no crypt-to-crypt lighting, it's going to be dark. I'm on the night crew, so I'm going to relieve Officer Kyle over there, but I'm not sure what you can do this late."

"An officer is missing."

"You're going to keep looking. And we're grateful. As I said, everybody loves the man."

"Of course—" Jackson began.

He broke off as a series of shots rang out, ripping through the quiet air of the cemetery.

He and the officer looked at each other, froze for a second, frowned, then turned to the wall and leapt over it, drawing their weapons as they did.

"Coming from the woods, there," Jackson shouted.

"Right. Hell, we've got no cover."

"Yes, we do. Stay between the tombs and the mausoleums," Jackson told him.

He was already heading for the woods, his mind on Angela and Patrick.

Fortunately, he quickly saw the two of them, despite the encroaching darkness. They were headed in the direction of the shots, carefully dodging tombs, rounding mausoleums, and skirting stones as they ran.

The shooter seemed to have two weapons, a semi-automatic among them. A single shot was immediately followed by a barrage of bullets.

As Jackson closed in on the others, he heard a sudden scream of anguish coming from the woods. Another shot slammed into a stone, this time a single shot.

Jackson reached the side of a mausoleum where Angela had taken cover.

"I think I got the hand wielding the semi-automatic," she told him.

"Where's Patrick?"

"One tomb back," she said and hitched a thumb. "The cops are moving into the woods, trying to wedge him in. We're holding the front, hoping to keep his focus here."

"Good plan," he said. "Moving," he told her. "Cover me."

She just stepped aside, taking aim at the woods as he hurried to duck behind the next largest tomb.

A single bullet flew wildly into the air. He nodded at Angela. She took another shot.

This time, he made it to the trees and began slipping through the oaks and the brush growing so richly in the area.

He honestly shouldn't have been surprised by what he found when he finally discovered the shooter.

The man—or woman—wore a sheet with cut-out eyeholes, a nose hole, and a macabre, painted-on mouth, complete with fanged teeth and dripping blood.

Halloween.

But Jackson saw there was more blood dripping down the length of the garment. And the person still held a gun in one hand. From the size of the hand and build of the body, the shooter appeared to be male.

The other side of the shooter's body seemed to hang limply. Angela had indeed managed to strike one of the man's arms, causing him to release the semi-automatic he'd been wielding.

"Drop the gun!" Jackson roared. "Drop it, now!"

The man didn't do as instructed. Instead, he aimed for his head but then lowered the weapon slightly.

Jackson heard Angela as she moved almost silently behind him.

"We can't let him shoot himself. We need to know what's going on. He could lead us to Whittaker," she murmured and nodded.

He knew she meant to step out and try to talk to the man. He would cover her. She was experienced. An expert—and capable. He nodded in return and whispered, "We need Patrick."

"He's close," Angela said.

"Stop!" she cried to the gunman as he started to raise the gun to his head again.

She stepped out from the cover of the trees, looking at their costumed ghost. "Don't. Please, don't. You didn't hit any of us. No one is dead or injured. You might do some jail time, but... please. Don't throw away your whole life. Life is precious. *Your* life is precious."

"My life is worthless now."

The voice was that of a man.

"No. No life is worthless," Angela called to him.

"You don't understand. You can kill me, or I can kill me. Better than—"

Patrick arrived. He touched Jackson's shoulder before holstering his weapon and stepping out to join Angela.

"Not armed!" Patrick said quickly, lifting his arms. "I think I know what you're trying to say. You're afraid of whoever you're working for or with. You're scared that what they'll do to you will be far worse than dying."

"I—"

Patrick took a step toward the man, and the gunman shifted to point his gun at Patrick.

"Hey," Patrick said, stopping with his hand in a placating gesture before lifting his arms again. "I just want to see your face. To see you without that sheet. Maybe we can help with that injury."

"Back away again," the man said.

Patrick did. After a brief hesitation, the shooter appeared to attempt to maneuver himself out of the sheet while maintaining control of his weapon.

"May I help you?" Angela asked him.

He started to laugh. "You. You, of all people. Sure. Um... don't forget, I have a gun," he warned.

"We know that," she assured him.

Jackson held his position, ready to fire if the lives of either of his agents were threatened. But Angela moved to the man and carefully pulled the sheet away from him.

His side dripped with blood. She had definitely struck him.

"You need medical help," she told him.

The man was in his early twenties with shaggy brown hair, a narrow face, and a slim body. He had the look of a nervous terrier.

Drugs, Jackson thought. *He needs a fix.*

It was lucky he hadn't hit anyone, even with a semi-automatic.

Yet still...

Jackson maintained his position. They needed the man alive. They tried to bring people in whenever possible.

They were law enforcement, not judge and jury.

But this time was especially important. Whittaker might still be alive.

The man shook his head.

"I need... I need..."

His words broke off as he collapsed. Angela caught him, easing him to the ground as best she could. "Medics. We need help now!" she shouted.

The woods came alive with police. They allowed the Krewe to take the lead, but offered backup if necessary.

Jackson holstered his weapon and hurried over to Angela to check the man's vitals.

"Not sure what he was on, but our country has been suffering from the huge supplies of fentanyl circulating through the drug trade. It's been mixed with just about everything: heroin, meth, cocaine, marijuana—you name it. Angela, rip up the sheet. We can use it to slow the bleeding."

"Got it," she said.

Jackson helped Angela rip enough fabric to make a proper tourniquet.

"Honestly, I don't think this young man is behind anything. I think he was simply drugged up and told to get out here and take out the agents and police. They probably threatened to withhold his drug. But he seemed to know what happens to those who go against whoever is in power," Jackson said.

"Right. It's amazing he could even hold a gun, much less two. Much less hope to *hit* anything," Patrick said. "I am willing to bet he's on fentanyl, though I don't know mixed with what. He's lucky he's still alive."

"He was expendable. Maybe they *expected* him to die," Angela said.

"Probably," Jackson agreed. "Which means we need to keep him alive. The EMTs are here. Hallelujah. They can at least get him to a hospital."

The EMTs carefully wound through the trees and foliage, carrying a stretcher, nodding as they arrived. Patrick rattled off the man's status and vitals and told them that he believed the man's collapse had been caused by fentanyl-laced drugs.

"The curse of the day," one of the medics said. "Great tourniquet. You likely kept him alive."

"Thanks. He needs oxygen, probably a transfusion—"

"Yes, sir. We'll be on the line with the ER doc."

"And I'll be with you," Patrick said.

"No one is—"

"You can take one person. Especially one who has gone through medical school," Angela said softly.

"Great, fine. One person. And a doctor. Good," the EMT said.

They all nodded, and Patrick turned to Jackson and Angela.

"I'll be at the hospital, hoping he wakes up. Won't do any good for all of us to sit around. Besides, Angela has something to show you."

Jackson looked at Angela. "It could be something or it might be nothing, I don't know," she said. "Still, Patrick is right. We won't do anyone any good just waiting. And Patrick and Kat are our medical specialists."

The EMTs were already moving with their patient, so Patrick hurried after them. One of the police officers who had hovered nearby came over to Jackson and said, "We're ninety-nine percent certain he was a lone shooter. We've been through the woods, too."

"I'm pretty sure you're right," Jackson said. "Someone put that young man up to this. Someone who hoped that one of us would shoot him. Thank you for clearing the area."

"No, thank you. That was a loose-cannon situation. Someone could have died. Anyway, we'll get back to our posts. Or rather, I'll fill out the paperwork while the others get back to their posts." He chuckled. "I'll eventually need someone from your office to sign off on the paperwork, too, but I'll at least get it started."

"Thanks."

The officer shook his head. "My officers will also make sure that no kids have snuck in, given it's Halloween time, and they think they have to be cool."

Jackson nodded. "Yeah, go figure. Running around in a cemetery. Great fun for Halloween."

The officer nodded grimly and moved on.

"Back to the Robertson tomb," Angela said. "Or at least near it."

He followed her. On the way, they saw the ghost of Colonel George Clayborn hurrying toward them.

"I leave for the morning, and all hell breaks loose," the ghost said. "You're quite all right? The place is a mess of shattered stones. Who did this?"

"A sad, addicted human—one being used by someone else," Jackson said.

"He's still alive. We're not sure if he'll stay that way," Angela said. "But we have hope. And if he lives, he *may* be able to help us."

"That is good. Excellent," Clayborn said. He shook his head. "War is bad enough, men and women who just want to raise their children but serve a different crown or country. But killing randomly, this..."

Clayborn stopped speaking and shook his head. "Such insanity to come to such a place," he added quietly.

"We will get to the bottom of it. And hopefully stop it," Jackson vowed.

"Yes, I believe you will do all in your power to see the evildoers are brought to justice," Clayborn said. "And in that regard..."

"You have something that will help us?" Angela asked.

"I'm not sure, quite honestly. But I spoke with my friend, Sergeant Mahaffey of the DC police. He joined us here about twenty-five years ago. He doesn't spend much time at the cemetery, prefers the old mansion where his family lives so he can watch over his adorable grandchild. I'm sorry, I digress. Anyway, Mahaffey told me there were some strange soldiers here, both on the Fourth of July and on Labor Day. He assumed they were honoring our lost service men and women from the early days to the present." He shrugged and continued.

"Said there were maybe six or seven of them, all dressed as soldiers from different eras in history. Mostly, they stayed by the Robertson tomb and held some kind of service near it. Candles, books. He said one man led the rite or ritual... whatever it was." He circled his hands.

"Apparently, they came twice—more the first time than the second. But Mahaffey didn't think anything of it. Compared to the craziness of Halloween, what could possibly be so strange about people praying and honoring lost soldiers?"

"The flag," Angela murmured, looking at Jackson.

"What flag?" Jackson asked her.

"Patrick and I saw it earlier. I believe it's been there a while. I didn't think anything of it before. I mean, as Colonel Clayborn said, it seems benign next to the goblins and ghouls and witches set up everywhere for this time of year. But I had a strange feeling... It looks like some kind of marker. And there's a recent grave near the flag."

"Show me," Jackson said.

"That group could have just set up the flag to honor one of the dead," Clayborn said.

"They could have, but this thing may also go a lot deeper than we know," Jackson added.

"Ah. I've heard a great deal about normally sane people losing their marbles. Still believing the earth is flat, or that outer-space aliens walk among us. Oh! And Martians are the ones really running the federal government. Do you think conspiracy theorists are involved?"

"Not so, I'm afraid," Jackson said. "After what just happened, I think the only conspiracy here is getting others to make sure that illegal drugs continue to flood the market. Let's see this flag." He turned to

Angela.

Angela led him to the flag. It was store-bought, the kind that went on sale right around the Fourth of July every year and was sold just about everywhere.

He pursed his lips and nodded.

"We need to dig," she said.

"We'll get over to the office and let them know, and then I'll get a crime scene crew out here," Jackson said.

"You think we might find more victims?" Angela asked him.

"I'm sure that's what you were thinking. Hard to say, though. Someone set up the bodies in the Robertson tomb as if on display. Like some macabre, would-be artist wanted them to be seen," Jackson said. "If there *are* bodies here, someone went to the trouble to conceal them."

"There was no guarantee anyone would go into the Robertson tomb," Angela reminded him. "I don't think the killer planned on Debbie Nolan going to the police and then telling the people at the office what she saw. He barely caught sight of her at the last minute. So, it's possible his artistry was only for himself. But if it is drugs, Jackson, more than one person may be involved. Maybe our drug dealer finds those who are vulnerable, like the shooter who was here today, and uses them."

Jackson nodded.

"So, you think while the ground was still fresh, they just got rid of those digging in against them?" Colonel Clayborn asked. "All this while pretending to honor the dead."

"Quite possibly," Jackson said and shrugged. He felt his phone vibrating and answered it quickly.

Patrick, calling from the hospital.

"Good news or bad news?" Patrick asked as Jackson answered.

"Go with the bad, putting you on speaker," Jackson said and hit the icon.

"No identification whatsoever on the shooter from the woods. I went over every piece of his clothing. Both jeans and T-shirt were from a national department store. Sneakers and socks the same."

"Good news, Patrick. Please," Angela said.

"Well, the good news is that Dr. Banyan, the doctor treating our guy, seems to be top of the crop. Our shooter is still alive, but will be in a medically induced coma for a few days. Hopefully, Banyan will be able to bring him out of it in about forty-eight hours, but his first priority is to preserve life."

"Of course. Ours, too," Jackson said. "So, we'll speak with him as soon as we can. We're going to need someone at that hospital—"

"Already covered. Will is here, and we're getting a local police officer in, too. I have lots of faith in both teams, but double duty seems to be the order of the day."

"Good calls all, Patrick. Thank you."

"You're both still at the cemetery, right?" Patrick asked.

"Angela and I. And Colonel Clayborn. I'm sorry you didn't get to meet in person, but—"

"I will get to meet him before this is over, I imagine. Anyway... Angela, I believe you need to be especially careful."

"Me? Why?"

"I don't really know. It's just something our unnamed shooter said when we were out there talking with him. He was surprised, maybe even humbled or touched, that you wanted to help him. He said, 'You. You of all people.' And he was talking to *you*, Angela."

"Okay, but..."

"I think someone sent him out there to target you specifically," Patrick said.

Chapter 7

Angela remained stoic, wishing Patrick wasn't quite as talented as he was. Why did he have to home in on that possibility?

She and Jackson had an amazing relationship. Naturally, they loved each other. They adored their family.

And his respect for her and others was among the many assets he possessed that had made her fall in love with him.

But now, he would worry.

She spoke calmly because she refused to be taken off this case.

"I hear what you're saying, Patrick. But I also believe they're after any and all of us who interfere with what's going on. What we need to do is get to the bottom of this. Now," she said.

Jackson looked intently at her as he spoke.

"We'll take all that into consideration, Patrick. Right now, I'm afraid we might have found more victims. We need to get a crew out here to do some digging. We'll be in after. Of greater importance, and I figure you're on this while sitting around the hospital, how are we doing on tracking the video from the time of Officer Whittaker's disappearance?"

"I'm going over the security footage from two neighbors' homes, but Jordan was headed out to the safe house when she decided to do some more checking on Debbie Nolan's neighbors. We both intended to take over as guards to protect Debbie, and she's still headed that way eventually, but she finally found an eyewitness who was at the grocery store earlier and got something. The witness's name is Betty Newfield, and she lives just two doors down. The woman saw a navy-blue SUV she'd never seen before out on the street in front of the townhouses.

And she said that someone was packing things into the back—among them, a large bundle. I'm checking traffic cams on my phone now."

Jackson heard rustling over the line. "Ms. Newfield told Jordan more. She believes the man driving was about twenty-five and had shaggy brown hair. Said he looked like a kid."

Angela looked at Jackson. "Patrick, that sounds like the shooter from the woods. The guy you're watching over at the hospital."

"It sure as hell does," Patrick agreed. "If so, there's probably a navy SUV out in the woods somewhere."

"All right, listen," Jackson told Patrick, "I'm on it. I will send other agents to the hospital and to be with Debbie. I want you and Jordan, Colleen, Mark, Ragnar, and the dogs—all three of them—out here in the woods. Keep in mind that this killer seems to be working, sometimes cheerfully, out in the open. Other times, they're hidden. Honestly, I believe they're utilizing the woods as a hiding or staging area."

Watching him speak, Angela nodded and wondered again what it was about the Robertson tomb that puzzled her. Something about it *haunted* her.

"I'll make the calls," Patrick said. "We'll be right there."

"I'll get the cops searching the woods until you get here, though I'm not sure we'll find that SUV."

"Because our drugged-out fellow wasn't bright enough or in any mental or physical state to have pulled off the kidnapping of a trained and experienced cop?" Angela said, and Jackson nodded.

"Someone else is on this," she continued. "Jackson believes there's a head on this snake, and a number of others are being used in his operation and disposed of in this cemetery when they've worn out their usefulness."

The ghost of Colonel George Clayborn watched them as they spoke, shaking his head all the while.

When Jackson ended the call, leaving Patrick to handle the organization of the teams from the hospital, the colonel spoke quietly.

"This is... my home. The place I was lovingly laid to rest in peace. I've been fine remaining, watching the world grow and change. Sure, watching it sometimes backslide, yet trying to see my descendants grow without it doing so. Hoping I might intercede somehow if there is danger. But this horror has been happening right here, and I have been of little help to you," he said.

Angela shook her head. "No, the flag bothered me, but it wouldn't have meant much of anything without you to tell us about the rituals and the people in military garb."

She glanced back at Jackson. He was on the phone again, likely on a conference call with their crime scene units and the cop in charge at the cemetery.

Jackson was exceptional at quickly and clearly explaining what was needed and why, and this was no exception. He ended the call but only smiled grimly.

"A team of diggers is on their way out here now. Please, Colonel. Do not berate yourself. You have been a tremendous help."

"Our people know where to come, right?" Angela asked.

Jackson nodded.

"Okay, well, I'm ready to start digging myself—"

"Something done much more easily when one has a shovel." Jackson smirked.

"Good point. But there are some broken stones around here. Though if we're not going to dig, we *could* head back to the woods and start looking for whatever trails there might be that could accommodate a car. Or determine if whatever is being done starts at the state road. People don't pay much attention to cars just parked by the side of the road."

"We'll have a lot of help here soon. We can go wherever you want."

"I know where all the possible trails are," Clayborn said.

"Then lead away," Jackson told him.

Clayborn nodded, and they retraced their steps back to the woods. Thankfully, their shooter earlier had not hit any human beings, but he *had* shattered and chipped many a historical tomb.

The groundskeepers would be busy for days to come. But that mattered little when they were still barely scraping the surface of what had gone on. And while the Robertson tomb itself had been used for a horribly heinous crime, Angela thought that Jackson likely felt the way she did: there was far more out there. Somewhere.

Perhaps in the woods.

They paused in a tiny clearing once they left the cemetery boundary. Jackson looked around. The foliage was heavy, and the trees abundant.

Back in the days before the European occupation of North America, the Indigenous peoples had made this area of Virginia home. And while they hadn't built churches, graveyards, or cemeteries in the area, they *had* lived in and hunted the woods.

Some of the pine-covered trails had been etched out of the wilderness by foot as the Algonquian people hunted and lived, making use of the rich timber to be found here, as well as the wildlife that provided food and clothing.

Decade after decade, nature lovers kept the trails intact. Some had been broadened, and others had been reclaimed by the trees and brush.

Following behind, Angela hoped she could get service and pulled out her phone. She watched her step, but she pulled up information on the architect of the Robertson tomb, Gervais Conte, that Colleen had sent over.

The man had designed many a historical home in the area, but when she perused the information on him, the first thing mentioned was their current crime scene.

Before designing the mausoleum for the Robertson family, Conte had never designed such a piece before. He had been known for home design in the Richmond area. And, pre-war, he had created mansions for the nobility and gentry alike, along with office buildings for some of the up-and-coming towns and cities of his time. He spent the years of the American Revolution back in France, and didn't return until the last days of the war. According to his daughter, who had accompanied him back to the then-Colonies, he had been honored to design the tomb for a man he admired so greatly. Someone who had helped to create the nation he would then call his home.

Angela glanced up from her phone. Jackson had paused to speak to someone on his phone. She knew he would tell her what was going on when he completed his call.

She looked back at her screen.

After the war, relocated permanently to northern Virginia himself, Conte went back into the business of designing homes. He was said to have created beautiful places, but the war was barely over, and the land was scarcely civilized. He created lookout posts at the homes he designed, as well as some of the country's earliest escape routes and bell-trigger alarms.

"Interesting," she murmured quietly.

"Angela," Jackson said.

She looked up and saw that he and Colonel Clayborn had stopped directly ahead of her.

"You were right," he told her.

"About what?"

"That was our crime scene unit. They found remains in the ground. Ones that don't belong there. Chuck Downing said that while he isn't a medical examiner, he believes the two bodies found might have been in the ground for a little more than three months. If he's right, and the ME coming in confirms it, the kills—if they are murders—likely took place at about the same time as or just before our John Doe number one went into the mausoleum."

"My God," she murmured. "Trust me. I didn't want to be right that someone has been on a murder spree. No bodies were discovered until those in the tomb, so our victims were still considered missing persons."

"We'll get them now," Jackson assured her. And she loved that even though they both knew that wasn't a guarantee, he sensed her need for reassurance and, like always, gave her what she needed.

"Tire tracks. Right here," he said, pointing. "I saw them when I stopped to get the phone. We will rip the woods apart. The killer has likely been using the trail. Creating diversions in plain sight and bringing in what he's wanted and needed from the woods."

His phone rang again as he spoke to her. He answered it while sweeping out a hand to better show her the tire tracks he had discovered.

He listened intently to whoever was on the call, frowning. He thanked the caller and ended the call to look at her.

"Kat just got information back on our first John Doe. It was Wyatt Lange."

"Wyatt Lange?" she repeated, surprised. As far as she knew, he was doing time in a federal prison. He'd shot a guard while taking part in a bank robbery eight years ago, nearly killing the man. The Krewe was called in when the three robbers took off with hostages. They had been instrumental in finding the robbers' hideout. Angela had testified at the trial and had been the one to play head games with him during the negotiations, attempting to get him to release the young woman he held. As she begged, pleaded, and reasoned to buy time, Jackson managed to slip in from behind and disarm the man.

He'd had a good defense, convincing his attorney that he'd been forced to take part in the robbery and that two other men had held him at gunpoint until the very end. He hadn't known then that they'd both been killed, and thus failed to convince a jury.

"Dead three months, and we didn't even know he was somehow out of prison?" she asked skeptically. "Is it really him? Did Kat...

double-check everything?"

"You're forgetting how long ago that case was," Jackson reminded her. "He was sentenced to ten years but made parole. He shouldn't have. And if he hadn't, he'd at least still be alive I imagine, albeit behind bars," Jackson said.

"How strange that he was among those murdered... here," Angela said. "Well, at least we know he's not the one after me for testifying for the prosecution, since he became a victim himself."

"We'll get his phone records," Jackson said.

"But that's interesting. If an ex-con was directly connected to a fired tech guy and a luxury plane flight attendant, then I think you're right. This has to be drug-related," Angela said.

She'd almost forgotten that the ghost of Colonel Clayborn was still with them until he spoke.

"The shooter in the woods. Yes, he was drugged to the teeth," he said. "But again, I don't understand how all of this happened with us seeing so little. Of course, as you know, we don't just hang around our graves feeling depressed, we..." He paused, grimacing. "We haunt our families. That's often why we stay. And still, how did we—how have *I* missed so much?"

"They've clearly been working it through these woods. I say *they* because we know someone else dropped off our shooter today," Jackson said.

"Yes, that's true. That would make a difference. We don't go wafting through the trees all that often," Clayborn said.

"There's something here," Angela said. "And I still think there is something about the Robertson tomb we haven't figured out yet."

"Angela," Jackson said quietly, "I asked for a medical examiner to go through the tomb and make sure the bodies match the records."

She shook her head. "No, that's not it. I don't think there were others that didn't belong there—besides those hung up on display. My theory is out there, I know, and I'm sorry, but something just... isn't right. Anyway, we know that—"

She broke off. The sun had *shifted*, and in the distance through the trees, she thought she saw a strange glint of light.

"Something's out here. Over there," she said and pointed.

A light moved. As she indicated the direction of the glint and color, it seemed almost as if the trees had widened and grown, blocking whatever it was.

But she had seen it.

She knew she had seen something.

"There's *something* there," she repeated with determination as she slid past Jackson.

Of course, he and Clayborn followed her as she wove her way through thickets and trees.

And she was right.

They stopped and stared for a minute.

They had found the navy SUV.

She and Jackson walked to opposite sides, looking into the vehicle. No one sat in the front or back seats, but there was something large and dark in the back compartment that they saw through the rear window. But all the doors were locked and the windows were up.

"We've got to get it open," she murmured and hoped against hope that Officer Whittaker wasn't beneath the blanket she saw.

Dead.

"Forensics will need to go over the vehicle, but this can't wait," Jackson said. He pulled out his Glock, flipped it around, and slammed it with all his strength against the back window. Again and again and again.

The window broke at last, and he found the button to cause the back hatch to open. Once it was up, he instantly pulled at the blanket to see what lay beneath.

It wasn't Officer Whittaker. It wasn't a man at all, but rather ten or so stuffed toys, ranging from panda bears to monkeys.

"That may be good," Angela whispered. "I want to believe that Whittaker is still alive. And I somehow sense that he might be, whether that's wishful thinking or not."

Jackson was already calling their discovery in, letting the involved Krewe know they'd found the vehicle that the neighbor had seen and stating it had been abandoned in the woods.

But seconds after he made the call, he received one in return. It was Patrick. Jackson put the phone on speaker.

"I got the information on the SUV. Someone stole it from a home in Maryland two nights ago," Patrick said. "We'll be there in a matter of minutes. I've got Jordan and Brybo. Mark and Colleen are a few minutes ahead of me with Red. And Ragnar is heading to his place to pick up Hugo. All of us and the dogs will be there within minutes."

"Wonderful," Angela called out. "We have the police, and we're out here, but there is nothing like a good canine to find a person—living or dead," she added unhappily.

"See you soon," Patrick said.

Jackson sighed. "I'll report the car to the forensic units, though they're likely going to be running thin on personnel with all our different crime scenes. But the local police are in on this, too, so maybe we can use theirs, and it will all get done. Quickly."

"Whittaker isn't in the car. We have to find the man," Angela said.

"Agreed. We'll go northwest. I'll let the others know which way we're headed."

They started to move through the woods. As Angela did, she noted several huge, beautiful elm trees.

Colonel Clayborn saw her eyeing them. "Beautiful, aren't they?" he asked her. "And rare today. I tend to forget decades, but I believe many died in the 1970s when that Dutch elm disease swept across the world. Obviously, these survived. And at their size, I'd say they are old, at least one hundred years old. Maybe more."

"The trunks are huge," Angela noted.

"Yes."

The branches of the trees created massive canopies that stretched over the trails. They blocked most of the remaining sunlight as night started to fall.

But one didn't look quite like the others. It appeared as if, perhaps, lightning had struck at some point, causing a split high in the tree, leaving a slice-of-pie-shaped area of branches to fall toward the ground at a strange angle.

"That tree..." she murmured.

"Yes?" the ghost asked curiously.

"I must get up that tree," she said.

Jackson turned to her, frowning. "You want to climb a tree? Now?"

"Jackson, look... look at the size of the trunk. And the way the branches are jagged and slanting. I think there's a break at the top. Please. I heard something about kids during World War II finding the remains of a woman in a tree trunk." She bit her bottom lip. "I'm trying to remember... Oh! It was in Worcestershire, in England during World War II. And it was an elm tree!" She smiled. "It might have even been this particular kind. Jackson, please, trust me. Give me a boost so I can grab that branch."

"Angela, I can—"

"Come on, please. I can shimmy up the tree quickly. You can give me a boost, but I don't know if I can lift you."

He shrugged, nodded, and walked over to her. "All right, a tree trunk. Well, it can't get much stranger."

He gave her a boost, and she was able to hike herself up, grab onto another branch, and move higher and higher, finally reaching the place where it appeared the trunk had been split.

It had been.

And there was a several-foot-wide opening that stretched downward about four or five feet. She carefully maneuvered herself around so she could get a good grip with her legs around one of the sturdy branches and looked down into the gaping hole.

Her heart slammed against her chest.

Because there *was* something there.

A man.

And she could only pray that he was still alive.

Chapter 8

"It's him, I think," Angela called down from the tree.

"Is he alive?" Jackson asked her.

"I don't know for sure. I assume they just got him up here and then let him fall into the tree," Angela answered. "I'm trying to get an angle where I can touch him."

"Just be careful. If you fall out of the tree, you'll be seriously hurt," he warned.

"You think?" She chuckled. "Seriously, though, I'm good. Don't worry. I have strong legs, great muscles, and good balance," she called back.

He smiled. Of course, she joked. She did that sometimes when she was worried or nervous. But she was probably right. He honestly wasn't sure how she did it between work, two children, and everything else, but she did maintain an exercise regimen—though most of them did.

That strength and agility could mean the difference between life and death, though no muscle in the world could stand against the lethal qualities of a gun.

"Careful, careful, careful," he called.

She had managed to get herself into some kind of pretzel-like position where she dangled over the hollow section of the tree. He saw her reach down, inching a little farther. And farther.

"He's warm!" she shouted back.

"A pulse?" Jackson asked.

"I—I'm not sure. And I'm not sure how—"

"That's okay. Reinforcements are on the way. Get back up safely and hold your position." He turned to the ghost, wishing at that moment that the Colonel was still alive—flesh, blood, and muscle that could give him the needed boost to grasp the first low branch on the tree.

"Jackson!" Thankfully, and in an incredibly timely manner, he heard a familiar voice. Turning, he saw that Mark, Colleen, and Red were hurriedly pressing forward through the trees to reach him.

"EMTs," he shouted to Mark. "We need them over here now! And I need a boost."

"Is Angela stuck in the tree?" Colleen asked, seeming confused.

"No. We're pretty sure Officer Whittaker is in the tree," Jackson said.

"Up *in* the tree?" Mark asked, sounding dumbfounded.

"No. Literally *inside* the tree," Jackson said. "I need help here. Get me up so I can reach Angela. Between us, we might be able to maneuver him out. What we really need is a ladder. When we reach the EMTs, we need to make sure that emergency services arrive with one."

"I'm on the call," Colleen said, pointing at her phone.

"And I'll get you up the tree." Mark put his hands into the shape of a basket.

Gallagher had what Jackson needed to reach the branch. Catching hold of the first, he hefted himself higher and reached Angela's position. She still dangled slightly but had raised herself as if she were doing an extreme sit-up. "How do we get him out?" she asked.

"Colleen is getting emergency services to bring a ladder. But if we can switch around, I may be able to reach down far enough to get a decent grip beneath the man's shoulders. Then you can help guide him. If we're lucky, I can hold him long enough to get him down to Mark. The EMTs will be here soon, but if we can get him out before they get here..."

"Every minute counts," Angela said. "I just hope we don't do more harm than good. We have no idea what his injuries might be."

Jackson nodded, and below them, Red barked excitedly. Out of the corner of his eye, Jackson thought he saw the man wedged in the tree trunk shift just slightly.

Was it his imagination? Or was the man indeed alive?

"Mark!"

"Yeah?"

"We're going to try to get him down to you."

"Got it. I'm here. I'm ready."

Jackson thought of himself as being in decent shape, and his idea had seemed sound. He was taller and broader than Angela with a better wingspan. And still, he strained to lower his arms into the tree trunk, and felt the burn in his legs as he used them to hang from the branch over the hole as Angela had before.

He prayed the limb would hold his weight, but despite the previous injury to the tree, the elm held, the branch a strong one.

Muscles Jackson didn't even know he had burned.

But then... success. He caught hold of each of the man's shoulders and then managed to get a grip beneath his arms.

As he strained and pulled, he felt sweat dripping down his face and falling into his eyes. Just when he thought he might have to give up the quest, the wedged body in the tree begin to inch upward.

"Now!" he told Angela, and she quickly reached out for the body, guiding it from the tree and the branches, aiming him toward Mark.

Thankfully, Mark wasn't alone anymore. Ragnar was at his side. Even with the men below, Jackson realized he would have to let the body drop for a few feet, but he knew his coworkers would catch him before he reached the ground.

Jackson let go, and Angela eased back.

The man fell, only to be caught by the two Krewe members and eased gently to the ground.

"Got him!" Ragnar shouted.

Hugo was there then, along with Red, both dogs barking excitedly. Their masters calmly shushed them, but Jackson was just glad his plan had worked.

Jackson saw the man wince at the sound of the dogs, and now saw in the light of the full moon that it was indeed Officer Whittaker. He wasn't conscious, but it seemed his senses were still working. He was alive, and there was hope.

"Hey!" Mark shouted up to Jackson. "You need some help? You two are adorable up there. You look like a pair of possums getting situated for the night."

"Or vampires!" Ragnar shouted.

"Funny, ha, ha!" Angela called to him.

"Seriously. We're impressed as hell," Ragnar said.

"Catch Angela. I'm going to ease her down," Jackson called.

"On it, just let go, Angela. We're here," Mark said.

Jackson grinned at Angela. They were still hanging upside down and probably *did* look like a pair of vampire bats.

"I'm going to catch your hands. Hold mine tight. We don't want to dislocate a shoulder here. Then I'm going to let you ease into a flip and then let you go."

"Like one of those trust exercises, huh?" she asked. "Sounds very Cirque du Soleil."

He smiled. "Kind of. You trust me and those guys down there, right?"

"With my life," she assured him.

Angela held tight, and she was strong. Her body didn't lose the tension at all. Now, it was as if she were doing an extreme pull-up, and he eased her slowly down and then let her drop. Ragnar caught her first, and he and Mark worked together to balance her until she could stand on her own two feet.

"You next, my friend," Mark told Jackson.

"I'm a hell of a lot heavier," Jackson reminded him.

"Wait!" Colleen, who had been sitting with Officer Whittaker, his head cradled in her lap, called out the word. Twisting in his absurd position, Jackson saw that Patrick, Jordan, and Brybo were hurrying into the area.

Patrick, however, didn't even glance Jackson's way.

"You found him!" he said, referring to Whittaker. He rushed to the man's side, and Jackson saw him pulling a syringe from the medical bag he had thrown over his shoulder.

"Patrick—" he began.

"They play with fentanyl. I have naloxone. It's a temporary antidote. I'm willing to bet my life on this."

He gave the man the shot he carried.

Seconds that seemed like hours ticked by. Even the ghost of Colonel George Clayborn looked on silently.

Then Colleen looked at her brother before all of them. "He's already breathing easier!" she cried.

"Great. Now, we can try to get Jackson out of the tree," Mark said.

"No need," Ragnar said. "Ladder and EMTs have made their way through."

And they had. Two men and two women carrying a stretcher and a ladder appeared. One pair went to quickly speak with Patrick and get Whittaker on a stretcher, and the other set the ladder up for Jackson to make an easy descent from the tree.

Once again, Patrick planned to accompany the EMTs and his patient. Jordan would take their car and Brybo and meet him at the hospital.

"We're keeping the hospital watch overnight, if that's all right," Jordan said. "Now we have two people who could be in danger, and we all know that killers have the ability to sneak into even ICUs dressed as doctors or nurses. And while the cops are there, and they're great—"

"We need to be on this. Your plan is solid," Jackson assured her.

Brybo barked as if saying goodbye, and Jordan hurried after Patrick and the EMT squad.

When they were gone, Mark looked at Jackson and then at Colleen. "How the hell did you find the man in a tree?"

Angela smiled. "Well, I think we've figured out a few things now. The rest is just my research and ability to retain knowledge." She smiled. "We know they're making use of these woods. They're doing a lot by more or less hiding in plain sight or disguising what they're doing, but... it all came down to this documentary I saw about some kids finding a corpse in a tree in England during World War II. So, I looked at the tree."

"Still. Remarkable," Colleen told her.

"At least we found Whittaker. Or I should say, Angela found him. And she's right. We still need to scour these woods. But we've been going for about sixteen hours straight now, and the only light we have is the moon. Thankfully, it's full. We need to begin fresh in the morning. Our crime scene techs and forensic crews have been working the cemetery, but those they're working on can't be helped. It's time for us to call it quits for the night."

"Right," Mark agreed. "I think the dogs can see in the dark, but we can't. So, damned good job in the end."

"And with Patrick being here with his quick fix, the man at least has a chance," Angela said. "I'd say sleep is in order."

"Let's do it," Jackson said.

"I will keep watch over the cemetery throughout the night when the crews leave," Clayborn ensured. "It's one benefit to being me. I don't need sleep."

"Great, thank you," Jackson told him. "All right, guys. Let's get the hell out of the woods."

When they finally reached the car and made their way home, it was late.

Once again, the kids were in bed.

"Thank God for Mary," Angela murmured.

"She really is a blessing," Jackson agreed. Inside, he made a point of telling her that and filling her in on what had been happening.

"I am so grateful you found the man. And as for the kids... no problem," Mary told them. "I love them, you know that. And I love being useful."

"Tomorrow will likely be another tough day," Angela said.

"And the day before Halloween, too," Mary said. "I just hope... well, I know you were planning a nice holiday event at headquarters for those in town. And you want to take the kids trick-or-treating. I mean, a party is no big deal, but I know how you love your children."

"We have amazing kids, but, yes, we try to keep them out of cases as much as we can," Jackson said. "Though we did meet and adopt Corby because of a strange case, and we're damn lucky to have him as our son because of it. But, anyway. Mary—"

"No matter what, I will see that the children get to wear their costumes, get to their school and daycare parties, and go trick-or-treating. Though I hope you're able to do it with them. Of course, you do employ many great agents. Still..." She paused, then looked at Angela. "This is your case." She shook her head. "It's remarkable that you found a man in a tree."

"All of us accomplished a lot today," Angela said.

"And while we all know that cases can take days, weeks, and even months," Jackson said, "we're grateful to be moving forward. And so grateful we have you."

"We're all lucky. I'm lucky, too," Mary said.

She left them, and Jackson suddenly realized that he was starving. "Hm. Think we have anything to eat in the kitchen?" he asked Angela.

"I don't know. What do possums eat?" she teased. "Or vampires. Yuck. Never mind. Let's go back to possums."

"Let's go back to people," he said.

"Right. Except I'm too tired to—"

"Peanut butter sandwiches?" Jackson said and enveloped her in a hug.

"Now there's a plan." She smiled and kissed him on the cheek.

They had peanut butter and jelly sandwiches and some chips. A meal quickly prepared, eaten even faster, and filling enough for the night.

"I wonder," Angela said, glancing his way and pretending to be serious as she set one of their glasses in the dish drainer.

"Yes?"

"Are possums monogamous? Do they have loving relationships?"

Jackson raised a brow and shrugged. "I don't really know. We'd have to look that one up. I'm surprised you don't already know." He winked. "I do know one thing, though. At least about vampires."

"What's that?"

"They love to bite necks." He prowled her way. "I mean, I guess loving vampires bite necks gently, but..."

"No biting until the shower." She started to back up.

He grinned and kept stalking toward her, picking up his pace.

"I'll beat you in tonight." She started toward their room.

He ran ahead, stripping as he went, but stopped quickly to lock up his weapon.

She was right behind him and caught hold of his waist, pushing him back and then hurrying ahead of him. He laughed, catching up as she shed the last of her clothing, secured her weapon, and stepped into the shower, turning the water on to a delightful downpour of muscle-soothing heat.

He hopped in behind her.

She turned to him, laughing.

"I won."

"You cheated."

"What?"

"Less clothing."

"You're just a sore loser."

"You think? Just for that, I am going to bite your neck."

She laughed and was quickly in his arms. He teasingly nipped at her neck, then half-bit and half-kissed her shoulder. Then their mouths were all but glued together as they stood beneath the hot spray, letting the heat and the water work out the tension of the day and the soreness in them, allowing them to forget. And to want nothing more than each other.

Jackson knew he was lucky.

He had intense days.

But he also had these times when love and the beauty of the night cleared the soul of the evil men could do.

Chapter 9

Angela knew Jackson was watching her as they drove to the hospital the following morning.

"You're feeling guilty about the kids?" he asked.

"Yes, and no. I can't help but feel that this case, this particular one, needs us. And I know we have Mary, and the kids will have a great time no matter what. It just seems to be something, somewhere, every Halloween."

"True. But sometimes, other agents, those without kids, get to handle the lunatics. I am the field head of this case, and I can—"

"No, Jackson. We need to stay on it. I still can't explain why I feel like I'm missing something at the cemetery, especially at the tomb. And even in the woods. The fellow who designed the tomb—Gervais Conte—was remarkable for his day. When he designed houses, they had primitive alarms, bells attached to doorways and windows. He had escape routes for those in mansions. Who knows what he might have built into that mausoleum?"

"Well, we can either reach out to those with a higher paygrade and try to get a way to legally maneuver ripping up the place or try to get permission from Benjamin Robertson."

"We should start by asking. But I am bothered by all the bits and pieces we're getting along this grisly trail of murder," Angela said and turned to him. "Regardless, I think you're right. I believe this involves drugs. Both our still-unidentified shooter in the woods and Officer Whittaker were dosed with fentanyl—either intentionally or not. Patrick was right on that, I'm certain."

Jackson nodded. He'd spoken with Patrick that morning. Officer Whittaker *had* been given an opiate laced with fentanyl. The killer—or killers—had probably assumed he would die from it and stuffed him into the trunk of the tree to rot there where no one could ever find his bones.

"He's come to a few times, but so far, he has no idea of what happened to him," Jackson said. "Patrick believes as Whittaker recovers and the drugs get cleared from his system, he may start to remember. But he doesn't know for sure. He said the last thing he remembers is watching his team on television. He has no recollection of anyone at the door or a window. He doesn't recall hearing any noise, nothing. He was just there, and then he woke up in the hospital."

"What about our shooter?"

"Still in a coma. I don't think we're going to be able to speak with him today, but we'll go on in, look at both men, and make sure we've got agents tag-teaming to watch over them."

She nodded.

He shook his head, then looked at her and smiled.

"I remain amazed."

"About what?"

"A tree. You found a man in a tree!"

"Hey, I like documentaries. You learn all kinds of cool stuff. Oh, by the way, there's also the internet. I did some quick reading this morning. The common ring-tailed possum *is* monogamous. They create their home together and look after their little ones as a couple. As for vampires, there are differing opinions, of course, but as far as I could find, and given what I've seen in the movies, vampires like to fool around."

"I guess we're possums, then."

"Hm. You like to fool around."

"True. But only with you."

She grinned. "Good answer. But... I don't know. It's a tough call. The possums sound like loving little creatures—other than the fact that they eat insects. But they only live for a handful of years. Vampires, well, if you go by legend, they live forever."

"Until they get a stake in the heart." He winked.

An unexpected giggle escaped. "True," Angela agreed as she smiled at him, appreciating her husband so much in times like this. Especially the levity he'd purposely brought to her worried mind.

They reached the hospital and grew serious as they headed in. Patrick and Jordan were seated in a hallway, their position between Whittaker's room and that of the still unknown shooter. There were police officers posted at both doors, too.

Jordan's head was on Patrick's shoulder, but she seemed to shake herself awake as Jackson and Angela arrived. She stood to greet them, along with Patrick.

"No change," Patrick said. "But Bryan and Bruce McFadden are going to come in and relieve us. Brodie McFadden is doing a shift at the safe house now. We'll take all the dogs back to the woods and see if we can find anything else there—or find any more of those trees that might be hiding something. The dogs will be especially helpful, though we're all still amazed that Angela found Whittaker."

"Documentaries," Jackson explained for her.

"So I heard. Anyway, we'll let the dogs use their expertise today. If that works with your plans, Jackson."

Jackson nodded. "Sounds excellent. Kat is working with our local MEs on the new victims discovered in the ground. And Will is working on identifications." He shook his head. "Tomorrow is Halloween. I hope like hell…"

"Yes, we all do." Angela smiled at Jordan and then said to her and Patrick, "No matter what, you two need to get some sleep tonight. Otherwise, you'll be worthless."

"By the way," Jordan said, "Debbie apparently asks for you anytime anyone goes to the safe house, Angela. I think she sees you as her lifeline now. Understandable, since you *do* have a great way with people. As for the sleep… your wish is our command."

"How cool. It's great to command," Jackson said.

Patrick laughed. "Well, you are our field supervisor. So tonight it will be nice to heed the command of sleep."

"There's Marie, the charge nurse. Come on. I'll introduce you," Patrick said.

They met Marie. Their shooter still could not respond, though the doctors believed they could soon bring him out of his coma.

Officer Whittaker was in and out, but at least his condition was stable.

"He was lucky you found him when you did, and even luckier you had a medical man on your team," Marie told them. "You are welcome to go on in. Of course, please do not upset my patient."

"We promise," Angela murmured.

Patrick and Jordan said their goodbyes and headed out. Jackson and Angela headed into Officer Whittaker's room.

His eyes were closed, and he appeared to be sleeping peacefully. Angela and Jackson quietly found another chair in the room and moved it closer to the bed, setting it by the one already there.

They sat in silence to wait, but they didn't wait long. Whittaker soon opened his eyes. When he saw them, he frowned but then smiled.

"Oh. You two... thank you."

"No, thank *you*," Angela told him quickly. "Thank you for always doing your duty. And for being a survivor."

"Well, I survived with a little help from my friends, as I understand it," Whittaker said. "But I'm going a little nuts. I can't remember what happened. I asked about Debbie, but they told me she's fine. Said she was in a panic when she couldn't find me, but that you or one of your people got to her before she could be attacked and possibly killed. She is such a sweet young woman. Guarding her was like the job from heaven. But I failed her."

"We know someone took you from the house and brought you into the woods in a stolen navy-colored SUV," Jackson told him. "And one of the men who took you is the fellow being guarded in the next room. He started shooting in the cemetery. He was so high on fentanyl-laced opiates he luckily didn't hit anything but dirt and stone. But we believe someone was with him. Someone drove that car to where we found it. And that person left his friend behind to kill, cause a commotion, and then die—or so we think they hoped."

"But he's in a coma," Whittaker said.

Angela nodded.

"Medically induced. Hopefully, they'll bring him out of it by tomorrow. From what I've been led to believe, you are both lucky. Fentanyl-laced drugs kill."

"We're very lucky," Whittaker said and shook his head. "It was... it was all fine. I'm not trained in any way in that kind of stuff, but I thought if I just kept talking to Debbie, she might remember something. You know, something she didn't tell anyone yet that might be helpful. We talked about Halloween, about the lunatics that get up to no good out there on the holiday. She described the costume the guy with the bloody knife who ran into the woods wore. I just kept thinking she might think of something else. That... talking was good. I kept feeling like I was missing something. But I didn't want to press too·hard, so I said it was fine. Told her she was welcome to go on up and get her laundry folded. That I was happy to watch the game. The last thing I remember was my team scoring and then... nothing. Until I woke up here."

Angela turned to look at Jackson. "I think we may need to speak to everyone again. We haven't prowled around at the cemetery's office much—"

"Patrick went through all their security footage. The only people we saw going in and out of the office were those we know should be there: Benjamin Robertson, Debbie, and others who have family plots or mausoleums in the cemetery," Jackson said.

"Still, it can't hurt to do some more talking and digging. And we should record everything, because many ears are better than two," Angela said.

"Agreed." Jackson nodded. "Jordan was right. You do have a way with people. Maybe Debbie will come up with something and feel safer with you there." He felt his phone vibrate and glanced at it, then looked at Angela. "Bruce and Bryan are downstairs and on their way up. Owen," he said, addressing the officer where he lay on his bed, "you know the McFadden family. We're leaving you in good hands."

"Go out there and get these creeps," Whittaker said and smiled. "I'm doing better every minute. They are even going to let my wife and kids up later, or so the doctor promised."

"That will be great," Angela said. "There is no better cure than the love of our families."

Jackson and Angela left the room, pausing just outside until the relief agents arrived. As they headed down to the car, Angela said, "Divide and conquer?"

"No, no, no. You're not crawling around a tomb alone—"

"I'm not. Patrick and the others—along with the dogs—are in the woods. You need to speak with Benjamin Robertson again and then that writer. Patrick said that when he listened to interviews, he thought those we talked to first seemed a little sketchy, as if they knew something they might not have known they knew. I'm going to let you feel all good and warm and cozy about me because I'm heading to the safe house. At least, let's start this way. They may find something in the woods, you may get something from Robertson or Jefferson Moore. And when we've both had some time to talk, we'll meet up again and figure out where to go from wherever we are then."

Jackson nodded. "Sounds good. I'll drop you at the safe house. And I think I'll ask Robertson and Moore to meet me out at the tomb. Maybe putting them together will help. Then, we'll call someone else in, and you and I can get moving in whatever direction we find we need to go."

She smiled and nodded.

He was glad to see Angela walk into the safe house, using the code and her fingerprint. As she arrived, the door cracked, and then opened. He saw that Brodie was in the house, as he'd been told. He came out, greeting Angela as she arrived, listening to her, shrugging, then heading toward the gate. He keyed himself out, reset the alarm, and walked over to Jackson.

"Hey. She said she wanted to be alone with Debbie for an hour or so. I'll come back, but if Angela wants to be with her, knowing Angela, I'm sure she's after something," Brodie said.

"All right. If you want to come with me, I'm headed to the cemetery. I'm going to try to get Benjamin Robertson and the writer, Jefferson Moore, out there."

"Sure. I'll come with you. Fresh eyes. I haven't been out there yet. Then you can drop me off back here. I'll take the watch until tomorrow morning."

"Sounds good."

"And Halloween's tomorrow," Brodie said wearily. He shook his head. "I loved Halloween when I was as kid."

"I'm hoping we'll all still love it this year."

"We can always hope. But this is one hell of a tangle we have going here. We think we're looking for a drug runner with special knowledge of the Robertson tomb. And we don't think Benjamin Robertson is involved?"

"The man puts on a good act, if that's what this is. But that's why I'd like to get him to the tomb with the writer."

"You think the author can draw out the truth about Robertson? He is supposedly an investigative journalist."

"Maybe. I'll make the calls," Jackson told him. "Patrick says every interview we've done has seemed a bit sketchy—either legit, or because people don't know what they know. Anyway, he and his team have the dogs out in the woods. We'll see what we can do at the tomb. And

Angela will see if she can get anything more from Debbie."

"Hopefully. She didn't seem much interested in me. She left me in the living room with the television and told me to make myself at home. Just asked me to please leave her be. Oh, but she did ask me if Angela was coming. I told her I didn't know, but if she really wanted to see her, I was sure Angela would come by. Anyway, let's give the others a go," Brodie said. He angled his head thoughtfully as Jackson made his calls.

Speaking with Robertson, Jackson made it clear that they would be looking into his family's tomb further, with or without his permission. And that it would be extremely helpful if he came out to possibly save a lot of disruption to the tomb.

Jackson heard the man swearing at him before the call ended.

Calling Jefferson Moore was a bit different.

"I can't wait to get back in that tomb!" the man told him. "So cool."

"Great guy," Brodie said sarcastically after Jackson ended the call. "Murders are taking place, but visiting a tomb sounds like great fun."

Jackson looked over at him. "Whatever gets him there."

* * * *

"Oh, my God. You're here! I'm so glad to see you." Debbie Nolan hugged Angela as if she were a long lost and beloved relative.

Angela hugged her in return. "Hey, it's okay. I assume they told you we found Officer Owen Whittaker. He's going to make it."

Debbie nodded, looking worried. "Yes, yes, but he doesn't know what happened, either. Well, I guess my house was easy enough to get into, but nobody will be getting in here with the gate and the alarm and the door alarm and... it's great when the dogs are here, too. But... hey, I wanted a visit from you more than anyone else."

"The Krewe is a unique unit of law enforcement," Angela assured her. "Each of our agents is excellent, qualified, and talented, and you are in the best hands possible with any of our people watching over you."

"I'm sure. I just... I just wanted you. Anyway, I think I should buy a dog. A big dog like one of the guys your agents have. A big Doberman, maybe. Or a Great Dane or an Irish wolfhound. What do you think?"

"I think it's a great idea if you want to take care of a dog," Angela said.

"I was going to make tea. Would you like some?" Debbie asked.

"All right. But, Debbie, what we really need to do is talk. I'd like to get you to lie down and close your eyes. Then I'll ask you some questions and tell you to think not just visually but with all of your senses. I keep thinking if the killer is coming after you, he thinks you know more than you do."

"It's not just random?" Debbie said.

"No. We got a shooter yesterday who was full of drugs laced with fentanyl. And when we found Officer Whittaker, he had drugs and fentanyl in his system, too."

"So, other than cops, this guy goes after junkies?"

"Maybe. Or maybe those who have helped him, who aren't so helpful anymore. We believe they intended for the shooter in the woods to die after he created the chaos."

"And you found Owen Whittaker."

"We did." Angela frowned. She'd just told her that.

"No, no. *You* found Officer Whittaker. In that tree! Who knows to find someone in a tree?" Debbie said, shaking her head with admiration.

"The important thing is that he is safe and well."

"Yeah, but he doesn't know what happened." She'd mentioned that already, too. Angela tried to keep her expression blank.

"This is crazy. I don't know how he was taken. He doesn't know how he was taken. There was a car, the car was abandoned, and he was in a tree." Debbie shook her head and headed into the kitchen. Angela followed, watching her put the kettle on to boil.

"We'll find out. Our people are there today with the dogs, tearing through the forest. Oh, and we dug up more older victims of whoever our unknown killer is. We are getting closer and closer. We will have answers soon."

"I believe in you," Debbie said. "Would you grab some cups? They're up in there on the left. Oh." She laughed. "You probably know. This is your safe house."

"I do know. And sure," Angela said, reaching for the cups.

Her hand raked over something sharp, and she frowned, looking down at her palm. No big mark, just a little scratch. She ignored it and said, "It's not so much believing in me. There is a whole system at work. Several teams are working different angles. And, in all honesty, that's why I'm here. Don't get me wrong, we seriously care about your safety. But we do need something from you. Special Agent Patrick Law is also Doctor Law. He specializes in... listening to and understanding people. He believes we didn't get everything we might be able to get from you."

"I thought... I thought they figured out it was drug smugglers or something. I don't do drugs."

"We're not saying you do. Hm, tea actually sounds good. I'm just going to go check to make sure I reset the alarm after coming in. I'm almost certain I did, but I was so happy to see you."

Angela gave her a smile and walked out of the room, wondering why the tiny scratch she'd received was making her feel unbalanced.

She quickly put through a call to Jackson.

He answered on the first ring.

"You okay?" he asked quickly.

"Fine, but I'd like you to get Patrick out here. I can't place anything specific, and she may just be chatty and nervous, but... Debbie Nolan knows something, and she's acting kind of odd. And... wow."

"Wow, what?"

"I scratched my hand getting some cups out of the cupboard. It's nothing. Just a scratch. But something seems off, and..."

There seemed to be a sudden wall of strange static in her ears.

And then...

Nothing.

Chapter 10

"Angela! Angela!"

There was no response. Jackson ended the call and tried ringing her again.

No reply.

"What's wrong?" Brodie asked him.

"Angela. Her line went dead."

"In the safe house? That's not really—"

"Debbie Nolan," Jackson said. "Angela said something seemed off and that she scratched herself on something. Brodie, I need you to stay here. I'm getting Patrick and going back to the safe house. Don't trust anyone but the Krewe, and don't get close to anyone. I'm going to get Mark and Colleen and Red over here. I really don't trust any of these other people. Patrick said every interview has been strange. But I need to get to Angela."

"Go. I've got this," Brodie told him.

Jackson ran out of the cemetery, calling Patrick as he did. He wasn't quite sure where Patrick was in the woods, but the man managed to get to him just as he reached his car, which was parked close, outside the cemetery wall.

And he'd come with Brybo.

"Angela said something was off with the way Debbie was talking. She couldn't put her finger on what it was. She also said she scratched herself on something in the cupboard, and she sounded strange. What the hell, Patrick? Could Debbie be the one behind all this?" he asked as the man and dog crawled into the car.

"Could she be? Yes. And if anyone could pull off something in a safe house, it would be the one staying there."

"But you can't get out without an alarm going off if—"

"Jackson. Your phone. That sounds like the warning alarm is going off at the safe house."

Jackson pulled out his cell.

And swore softly. There had been no car there. Debbie hadn't brought one. He had dropped Angela off in his. But they had gotten Officer Whittaker out of Debbie's house.

They could get Angela out, too.

And Debbie Nolan clearly had help.

"We worried about protecting the woman who caused the whole thing. And now she knows Owen Whittaker is alive, and her shooter is alive. She needs both of them dead. But why Angela?"

"She's been a target. I don't know why, but she's been a target all along," Patrick said.

"There has to be a reason. And there has to be some connection to the other victims."

"Angela testified against the one man, but he's among the dead. Maybe she didn't want him to be. This girl, though..." Patrick said.

Jackson put through a call to the team at the hospital and then called the office, asking for the tech department and saying it was crucial. They needed everything they could get on Debbie Nolan. Immediately.

They reached the safe house, and Jackson headed straight for the computerized lockbox. But before keying in his code, he noted that the gate wasn't fully closed.

He drew his gun. Patrick did the same. With Brybo running ahead of them, they approached the house.

The front door was also ajar.

Jackson stepped inside.

"Angela!" There was no answer.

"Upstairs," Patrick told him, running up the staircase. Jackson tore into the kitchen. Cups had been set on the table, and a teapot was there with sugar, creamer, and plates.

A kettle sat on the stove.

But there was no one to be seen.

He grabbed a chair and hopped up to see inside the cupboard. A nail protruded—one he was sure didn't belong there. One that had been set in place, likely by Debbie Nolan.

"Clear!" Patrick shouted from upstairs.

"Clear!" he shouted in return.

Patrick came back into the kitchen with Brybo. The dog whined, sitting anxiously.

"She got her out somehow. Just like she must have drugged Whittaker and got him out of her house," Jackson said. "It got tougher here, but beg for a specific agent, be the poor terrified victim desperate for help, and you could play the game again. Though she has to know now that we know, so..."

"She's doubly dangerous," Patrick said. "But, Jackson, what we have to do is find Angela. Debbie doesn't shoot people. She slices throats, but she hasn't played with her victims. If she's the one doing the killing. She figured the tree would kill Whittaker—"

"So she won't make the same mistake again," Jackson said. "Except if she has a thing with Angela, she won't want to kill her too quickly. I'm betting she can't believe Angela found Whittaker in the tree. She'll need to prove she's cleverer. So..."

"Angela is definitely alive," Patrick said. "We just have to find her."

"And she's in that cemetery—or the woods. Somewhere," Jackson said. "Brybo! We've got to go. Find Angela!"

Brybo barked, and they headed out of the house.

Jackson got a call back from Michael Banyan in the tech department and put the phone on speaker.

"We couldn't find anything on Debbie Nolan," Banyan told Jackson. "But I thought about Angela and what Debbie would likely do next. I realized she would have looked for a name change a while back. We researched that and struck gold. Debbie Nolan is really Jennifer Tanner. Her father was a drug runner the Krewe played an essential part in putting away. In fact, Angela was the one to figure out that he was heading into a Miami harbor, and the Krewe and the Coast Guard caught up with him there."

"It's revenge," Jackson murmured. "It's revenge, plain and simple. All right, put an APB out on her and Angela. Video from everywhere—"

"On it, sir," Banyan promised.

Jackson looked at Patrick and gunned the car as he took in the day.

The sun was already setting.

And they were returning to the old cemetery surrounded by woods. They'd have an hour of dying sunlight left if that, beautiful golds and mauves already streaking across the heavens.

Then, darkness would descend.

Light or dark, they *would* find Angela. Because she was still alive. He didn't know why, but he was sure in his heart that if she wasn't, he would know.

* * * *

Angela reached out, inching her way along the stone of her strange prison. Memories were returning, bit by bit, and then in a rush.

Suddenly, they seemed to flood into her mind. She remembered all of it.

She'd been drugged.

The scratch hadn't been just a scratch. Whatever little piece of metal had snagged her had been set in the cupboard on purpose and laced with something.

Knocking her out just enough to get her out of the safe house.

Making her compliant enough to get her to wherever she was... but not enough to leave her unconscious for a long time or dead. No, Debbie wanted her to suffer and know that she was far more cunning than any Krewe member.

Well, she had been. She'd played the ultimate victim.

What was more benign than a cup of afternoon tea?

But why? Why give herself away? She might have gotten away with all this so far, but she would have to know once she was out of the safe house, the Krewe would be on to her.

Angela was startled to hear a voice, muffled and from some distance. It was Debbie's voice, and she sounded delighted.

"I'm betting you're awake by now! Ah, Angela, clever Angela who does all her research, who figures everything out. Well, you're awake, and now you can crawl around in the dark for eternity. Of course, when they find me—"

"They'll arrest you," Angela said, her voice surprisingly strong.

"Me? Little old me? Poor girl, her defender taken once, and then the woman sent to guard her useless and incompetent, causing her to be abducted again, knocked out, only to wake in the darkness of the woods and escape in terror."

"Debbie, there are cameras all over that house."

"There *were* cameras. All disabled now. You know, I was almost part of Robertson Technologies. But, anyway, I'll just be so pathetic when they find me..."

"I already told Jackson you were guilty," Angela said. She was exaggerating, but Jackson would have known once she went silent that something was wrong.

And she had said that she felt Debbie knew something and was acting strangely.

"You bitch!" Debbie said. "You are going to die in the darkness all alone and screaming, but no one will hear you! Die, like you made my father die."

"I made your father die?"

"You put him in prison. And he died there!"

Who is her father? Does it matter?

"Well, maybe you'll die in prison, too," Angela said quietly.

"Bitch!" Debbie cried. Then... nothing. Angela knew that wherever Debbie had been, she was no longer. Only the darkness was there. The stone below her was cold, and she closed her eyes against the darkness for a minute. They were by the woods or in the cemetery.

She had known there was something wrong with the crypt. It clearly had an underground catacomb, and she was in it.

There had to be a tunnel that led to the woods. Maybe Gervais Conte had not been the one to build it. Still, she was suddenly certain she had figured it out. Debbie and her accomplice or accomplices had carried out their murders in the woods and used the tunnel to bring the dead into the cemetery.

All she had to do was...

She touched something and moved her fingers over it.

Suddenly realizing that it was bone.

Yes, she was in a crypt, or rather the space beneath it. Likely some kind of catacombs or something. There had to be a tunnel, and Debbie had been in it when Angela had heard her speaking.

There was a way in. Therefore, there was a way out. And Angela would find it.

Because she was going to live. As she began to crawl, she heard another voice. "Angela, Angela! I'll get to Jackson. I've found you, oh, hallelujah! You're going the right way, doing the right thing. This stretches from the crypt to the woods. But I didn't know it. Keep going, keep going, keep going..."

"Colonel?" she whispered in the darkness.

"At your service, ma'am."

* * * *

"There is something else in this crypt?" Benjamin Robertson asked, his expression one that appeared to offer real confusion. "I came here with my folks, even as a kid, because my however-many-times-great-grandfather was a hero and I had to know it," he said, making a pained face. "I just don't..."

"You don't know how people got into it either, right?" Jackson asked him.

Robertson sighed, looking down. "Me, I guess. I don't know. My father was old and sick, but he was still my father. The day of the funeral... I was off. I don't know. Maybe I left it open. Who the hell wants to admit they might have been an unwilling accomplice to murder?"

"Now that sounded like the truth," Brodie said dryly.

Jackson was there now with Robertson, Brodie, and Patrick. And Brybo. Jackson was glad that Brybo was with them.

Robertson kept a nervous eye on the dog.

And Jackson needed to know what the man knew about the tomb.

"Are there three graves under the floor?" he asked.

"I'm telling you, if there are, I don't know anything about them."

Jackson stared hard at the man. He felt his phone vibrating and quickly answered it.

Mark was on the other end.

"We're out here in the woods, and the dogs are going crazy. Someone is definitely out here. Not Angela, but maybe..."

"Someone who can lead us to her," Jackson said. He glanced at Brodie. "Heading to the woods. I'll have you gentlemen keep Mr. Robertson here company."

"Am I under arrest?" Robertson asked.

"Only if you attempt to leave," Jackson told him. He looked at Brodie. "The writer's a no-show?"

"Haven't seen him yet," Brodie said. "I tried his phone. No answer.
"

"Right. I'll be back."

Jackson ran across the graveyard at full speed. While the woods were dense and darkness was falling, he didn't need directions. He heard

Red and Hugo barking and howling up ahead, sounding as if in pursuit. Following their woofs and growls, he chased after them and found them at the base of a tall oak with wide-spread branches.

Mark and the others ran up just as they reached the tree.

"Get the hell down from there!" Jackson shouted.

"Oh, my God! You're yelling at me. That horrible man came, and he made Angela believe he came to tell her something important. She let him in and... oh, God! I don't know what he's done with her, but... I'm so scared. And now the dogs are after me!"

"We're here now, Debbie. You can come on down safely. We've got the dogs!" Jackson called out.

"I'm scared!"

"It's all right. You have to tell us about the man. We need to find Angela."

"I don't know... I don't know what he's done with her. And he's probably gone, anyway. He's probably run away, and... I'm so scared. I can't believe all this horrible stuff is happening to me!"

"Come down, we're here. We'll protect and help you," he called.

He heard shuffling. A minute later, Debbie dropped to one of the lowest branches and then to the ground. She had tears in her eyes and a pathetic expression on her face as she looked at him.

"Mark, would you be so kind as to arrest Miss Jennifer Tanner?"

The young woman's expression changed immediately and she turned to run.

"Red, Hugo, go for her!" Jackson said.

Barking, the dogs ran off obediently. Red threw himself onto the woman and plopped his weight down on her back while Hugo stood nearby on alert, watching for any attempt to escape.

The woman screamed with rage. Mark secured her and put her hands in cuffs, dragging her to her feet.

"Where's Angela?" Jackson demanded.

"You'll never find her. I'll die before I tell you. You can let the dogs chew me to bits, and I still won't tell you. She's going to die. That bitch is going to die. Who the hell finds someone in a tree? She's a witch and a bitch, and she made my father die—"

"Your father died," Brodie said, "because he was trying to shank another prisoner, and someone jumped on him instead. Not to mention the number of people he killed with his drugs, right?"

"You've brought it up a step, though. Killing your accomplices and clients with fentanyl if they stopped obeying or reneged on the money," Jackson said. "Where. Is. Angela?" Jackson said again.

"Slice me to ribbons. Oh, wait, you can't. You're cops," Angela said.

"We are agents," Jackson said. "But you're right. Of course, the dogs don't really know they're law enforcement. Patrick, these guys never swore an oath, did they?"

"I don't care. I'll never tell you where she is. She is going to die. You'll never find her!"

"Well," a strong, feminine voice said suddenly.

It was Angela's voice.

And she walked into the small clearing by the tree, filthy and ragged but standing straight and apparently unharmed. She smiled at Jackson, seemed to stop herself from running to him, and addressed the woman he now knew to be Jennifer Tanner instead.

"They're not going to have to find me because I'm not lost anymore."

"But you will be dead!" another voice suddenly raged.

Jackson swung around, at the ready. He'd known. He'd known because the man had said he was coming to the tomb and hadn't. He'd been busy.

Helping Debbie do whatever it was they'd done with Angela. She'd needed help. Just as she would have needed help getting the bodies into and hung in the crypt.

Jefferson Moore had a gun. And he raised it, ready to fire.

But Jackson had been in law enforcement for the majority of his adult life.

And he was faster. He didn't even have to kill the man, just shoot the gun out of his hand.

Screaming and wailing, the man fell to the ground. Heedless of the dogs and the cuffs now binding her wrists, Jennifer Tanner crawled her way to him, sobbing, thanking God that he was alive, promising him they would get off and everything would be all right.

"Well, go figure," Patrick said. "I do believe we owe Mr. Robertson an apology. But in the weeks to come, we'll have a lot of digging to do."

"We'll get these guys out of here," Mark told Jackson and Angela. He smiled at Angela and told her, "You need a bath."

"I do. And in the next few days, we'll get on clearing out the tunnels. But tomorrow is Halloween. Trick-or-treat. Though I think

Miss Tanner gets the trick this year. We get the treat." She turned, and Jackson saw that the ghost of Colonel George Clayborn was with her. "Thanks to a little help from our good friend, Colonel Clayborn."

"She's seeing a ghost. She's nuts. She's not right!" Jennifer Tanner raged.

"Oh, get her out of here. Please," Jackson said.

"With pleasure. Thank you, Colonel Clayborn," Mark said. He grabbed hold of the writer, Jefferson Moore, who was screaming that he needed medical help. Ragnar and the others followed, and the dogs obediently ran along.

"I need to call Brodie quickly and tell him to let Robertson go. And then... well, Mark is right. You really need a bath. Still..."

Jackson paused, looking at the ghost. "She is amazing, right?" he asked.

"Special Agent Angela Hawkins Crow would have gotten out with or without me, but it was a pleasure to help. I know why I'm here. You will keep visiting and ask me for help when needed?" he asked.

"Oh, sir. Yes, indeed," Angela promised. "Those guys can do the paperwork. I'd love to go home and have a shower."

They bid the colonel goodnight and headed out. At the car, however, Jackson had to stop. He held her tightly for just a minute. He was so grateful to have her in his arms.

She held him in return. They didn't talk.

They made it home just in time for the kids to be going to bed.

They also informed Angela that she needed a bath. She laughed and agreed once more but added that she'd had to play a bit in the ground for her, Daddy, and the Krewe to catch the bad guys.

"But we all get to do Halloween?" Corby asked excitedly, with Victoria echoing him.

"You bet," Angela promised.

Dirty and all, she hugged her children and told Jackson that she'd get them to bed. They said goodnight to Mary, thanked her again, and assured her that the Halloween party the next day was on.

Jackson felt his phone vibrating and headed into their bedroom to answer it. A few minutes later, Angela came in, and he told her about the conversation he'd just had with Patrick.

"Mark, Colleen, and our wonderful Krewe members have been on paperwork duty, and Patrick had a very interesting conversation with Mr. Jefferson Moore. He discovered that it wasn't the proclaimed architect who made the adjustments to the tomb, but a Robertson during the Civil War. He created the tunnel beneath the crypt that led to the forest as part of the Underground Railroad. When *Debbie Nolan*, as we knew her, lost her father, she set her mind on revenge. And using his drug business gave her an edge. She recruited followers to help her get the drugs out and make the money needed for her ruses, and when they got in the way, she used new recruits, strung out and desperate, to kill the people jeopardizing their livelihood. The victims, we'll discover, were in on the sales—junkies. She used a lot of fentanyl to get rid of people who had outlived their usefulness, too. What she wanted in the end was to get to us. Starting with you. But... she wanted to punish the FBI in general. She was both sociopathic and a damned good actress."

She nodded. "So, they've done the paperwork?"

"Well, they're *doing* the paperwork. We'll have a lot of pieces to finish up. But the way things seem to be going, we'll have a lot of work tomorrow morning..."

"And then Halloween. A good, fun one. Finally."

"You got it."

She smiled at him for a minute and then said, "Ick! All right! Shower! Hey, that's the first time in my life several people have told me that I needed a bath."

"Well..."

She smiled and bee-lined for the bathroom. Jackson gave her a minute and then joined her.

At first, they smiled and ran soap over each other.

He had to keep holding her.

They finally made it into the bed and made love.

And he held her throughout the night. Maybe they were lucky. Perhaps they knew how to appreciate the simple things like sleeping together. Because they knew how quickly it could all be taken away.

Holding each other tight, they slept.

And morning came.

Jackson woke first, leaning up on an elbow just to watch her sleep.

Her eyes opened, dazzling and beautiful.

And he smiled.

"Happy Halloween!" he said.

She laughed. "Yes, Happy Halloween."

Epilogue

Angela was delighted. For a moment, she simply closed her eyes and then reopened them.

The world was full of light.

Laughter and music surrounded her.

Best of all, she was alive and well. She was with both her family and her extended family. And the world, as she had always known and appreciated it, was a beautiful place.

And, remarkably, tonight they could celebrate.

The Krewe Halloween party proved a big success. Everyone from every floor gathered in the largest conference room and the reception area. They tried to have something for each of the holidays, big or small. Many agents were away, working cases across the country and beyond, but whoever was in town and free was always welcome to join.

That included Mary, who was there with her beloved nephew, Agent Axel Tiger.

Adam and Jackson had decided from the first days of the Krewe that the concept of family would be important to the group.

They'd ordered in a nice supply of food for tonight. Halloween, while not yet Thanksgiving, was still a good time for a main course of turkey. For the pescatarians, there was grilled salmon, the vegans had tofurky, and for the vegetarians, a pasta dish filled with vegetables.

Everyone had been invited to bring their children, so there were plenty of candy bowls.

Of course, Angela had also come up with treats of fruit snacks, apples, and mini-protein bars, a little healthier than the candy, but it *was* Halloween.

A cake had been crafted to look like a Jack-o-lantern.

However, there were no dangling skeletons or the like to be found around the office.

They'd had a bit too much of the real thing recently.

In unusual fashion for their son, Corby had opted to be a superhero this year rather than any kind of a ghoul or monster. Little Victoria was delighted to run around as a mermaid.

Angela had decided to wear a Disney costume. One that allowed her to represent her favorite storybook character: Maleficent.

Someone had teased Jackson about bringing out his father's old ceremonial clothing, but he'd said it had just felt right.

Will, who had been an actual magician and illusionist before joining the Krewe, returned to his roots. As *Merlin,* he spent much of the night entertaining the children and adults alike with his tricks.

The night came to an end, and Jackson's last speech for the event, as was customary, was his thank you to his team.

He told them that it didn't mean they had to go home. *He* just had to go home—that's what happened when you had kids in the house.

His words, as intended, were met with laughter, and then there were a bunch of goodbyes. In no time, they were finally out of there with the kids and then back at home. And though it took a bit—the kids had enjoyed a truly wonderful day at school, in the neighborhood, and at the party—they finally got Corby and Victoria to bed for the night.

Then, it was time to be together.

Sometimes, they talked about their cases.

But not that night.

Tonight was just for gratitude.

"There's nothing I love like a good fairy who can be the toughest woman in the universe as well," Jackson said as he swept her into his arms. Her Maleficent horns fell to the floor, and the rest of their costumes soon followed.

She had just one reply.

"This is so much more comfortable than a bed of stone."

He smiled and pulled her more tightly against him.

"My love, I would sleep with you anywhere. Then again, we did buy a good mattress."

She grinned, and they kissed.

Soon, Halloween was history, and yet it was one to remember for both the fear and the wonder of the teamwork and training that let them all survive—and conquer.

Then there was being with Jackson.

Making love.

And loving.

* * * *

Also from 1001 Dark Nights and Heather Graham, discover Haunted House, The Dead Heat of Summer, Blood Night, Haunted Be the Holidays, Hallow Be The Haunt, Crimson Twilight, When Irish Eyes Are Haunting, All Hallows Eve, and Blood on the Bayou.

Sign up for the 1001 Dark Nights Newsletter
and be entered to win a Tiffany Key necklace.

There's a contest every month!

Go to www.1001DarkNights.com to subscribe.

Discover 1001 Dark Nights Collection Nine

DRAGON UNBOUND by Donna Grant
A Dragon Kings Novella

NOTHING BUT INK by Carrie Ann Ryan
A Montgomery Ink: Fort Collins Novella

THE MASTERMIND by Dylan Allen
A Rivers Wilde Novella

JUST ONE WISH by Carly Phillips
A Kingston Family Novella

BEHIND CLOSED DOORS by Skye Warren
A Rochester Novella

GOSSAMER IN THE DARKNESS by Kristen Ashley
A Fantasyland Novella

DELIGHTED by Lexi Blake
A Masters and Mercenaries Novella

THE GRAVESIDE BAR AND GRILL by Darynda Jones
A Charley Davidson Novella

THE ANTI-FAN AND THE IDOL by Rachel Van Dyken
A My Summer In Seoul Novella

CHARMED BY YOU by J. Kenner
A Stark Security Novella

THE CLOSE-UP by Kennedy Ryan
A Hollywood Renaissance Novella

DESCEND TO DARKNESS by Heather Graham
A Krewe of Hunters Novella

BOND OF PASSION by Larissa Ione
A Demonica Novella

JUST WHAT I NEEDED by Kylie Scott
A Stage Dive Novella

THE SCRAMBLE by Kristen Proby
A Single in Seattle Novella

Also from Blue Box Press

THE BAIT by C.W. Gortner and M.J. Rose

THE FASHION ORPHANS by Randy Susan Meyers and M.J. Rose

TAKING THE LEAP by Kristen Ashley
A River Rain Novel

SAPPHIRE SUNSET by Christopher Rice writing as C. Travis Rice
A Sapphire Cove Novel

THE WAR OF TWO QUEENS by Jennifer L. Armentrout
A Blood and Ash Novel

THE MURDERS AT FLEAT HOUSE by Lucinda Riley

THE HEIST by C.W. Gortner and M.J. Rose

SAPPHIRE SPRING by Christopher Rice writing as C. Travis Rice
A Sapphire Cove Novel

MAKING THE MATCH by Kristen Ashley
A River Rain Novel

A LIGHT IN THE FLAME by Jennifer L. Armentrout
A Flesh and Fire Novel

Discover More Heather Graham

Haunted House: A Krewe of Hunters Novella

Halloween! Strange things are going to happen and every year, while loving the holiday, members of the Krewe of Hunters also dread it.

Something somewhere is bound to happen.

And it does.

Krewe member Jon Dickson's fiancée Kylie Connelly is contacted by an old friend who has just moved to Salem, Massachusetts, when the unimaginable happens as the holiday approaches.

Jenny Auger has just managed to buy the historic home of her dreams. But it comes with far more history than she ever imagined—the skeletal remains of seven victims interred in the old walls of the house years and years before—along with a threatening curse.

And strange things are happening in the city. Bizarre attacks…murders that mimic days of old.

With Halloween on the way.

Kylie has a history with the city of Salem, and her strange talent for being within the minds of those under attack—first realized in the city—remains sharp.

But the situation is far more dire than what they have discovered, with strange events and attacks occurring.

And with all their talent for crime solving—with help from the living and the dead—it still remains to be seen if they can solve the murders of the past before Halloween, and the bloodbath that just might occur if the sins of a time gone by cannot be brought to light.

* * * *

The Dead Heat of Summer: A Krewe of Hunters Novella

Casey Nicholson has always been a little bit sensitive, and she puts it to use in her shop in Jackson Square, where she reads tarot cards and tea leaves. She's not a medium, but she *can* read people well.

When the ghost of Lena Marceau comes to her in the cemetery, shedding tears and begging for help, Casey's at first terrified and then determined. Lena knows she was the victim of a malicious murder. Assumes her husband was, as well, and now fears that her daughter and sister are also in danger. And all over what she believes is someone's quest to control Marceau Industries, the company left to Lena's late husband.

Casey isn't sure how she can help Lena. She isn't an investigator or with any arm of law enforcement. But when she receives a visit from a tall, dark and very handsome stranger—ironically an FBI agent—she realizes that she's being drawn into a deadly game where she must discover the truth or possibly die trying.

Special Agent Ryder McKinley of the Krewe of Hunters has his own strange connection to the case. Hoping to solve the mystery of his cousin's death, he arrives at Casey's shop during his hunt for answers and finds something wholly unexpected. He fears that Casey's involvement puts her in danger, yet she's already knee-deep in deadly waters. Unfortunately, there's nothing to do but follow the leads and hope they don't also fall prey to the vicious and very human evil hunting his family.

* * * *

Blood Night: A Krewe of Hunters Novella

Any member of the Krewe of Hunters is accustomed to the strange. And to conversing now and then with the dead.

For Andre Rousseau and Cheyenne Donegal, an encounter with the deceased in a cemetery is certainly nothing new.

But this year, Halloween is taking them across the pond—unofficially.

Their experiences in life haven't prepared them for what's to come.

Cheyenne's distant cousin and dear friend Emily Donegal has called from London. Murder has come to her neighborhood, with bodies just outside Highgate Cemetery, drained of blood.

The last victim was found at Emily's doorstep, and evidence seems to be arising not just against her fiancé, Eric, but against Emily, too. But Emily isn't just afraid of the law—many in the great city are beginning to believe that the historic Vampire of Highgate is making himself known, aided and abetted by adherents. Some are even angry and frightened enough to believe they should take matters into their own hands.

Andre and Cheyenne know they're in for serious trouble when they arrive, and they soon come to realize that the trouble might be deadly not just for Emily and Eric, but for themselves as well.

There's help to be found in the beautiful and historic old cemetery.

And as All Hallows Eve looms, they'll be in a race against time, seeking the truth before the infamous vampire has a chance to strike again.

* * * *

Haunted Be the Holidays: A Krewe of Hunters Novella

When you're looking for the victim of a mysterious murder in a theater, there is nothing like calling on a dead diva for help! Krewe members must find the victim if they're to discover the identity of a murderer at large, one more than willing to kill the performers when he doesn't like the show.

It's Halloween at the Global Tower Theatre, a fantastic and historic theater owned by Adam Harrison and run by spouses of Krewe members. During a special performance, a strange actor makes an appearance in the middle of the show, warning of dire events if his murder is not solved before another holiday rolls around.

Dakota McCoy and Brodie McFadden dive into the mystery. Both have a. special talent for dealing with ghosts, but this one is proving elusive. With the help of Brodie's diva mother and his ever-patient father—who were killed together when a stage chandelier fell upon them—Dakota and Brodie set out to solve the case.

If they can't solve the murder quickly, there will be no Thanksgiving for the Krewe...

* * * *

Hallow Be the Haunt: A Krewe of Hunters Novella

Years ago, Jake Mallory fell in love all over again with Ashley Donegal—while he and the Krewe were investigating a murder that replicated a horrible Civil War death at her family's Donegal Plantation.

Now, Ashley and Jake are back—planning for their wedding, which will take place the following month at Donegal Plantation, her beautiful old antebellum home.

But Halloween is approaching and Ashley is haunted by a ghost warning her of deaths about to come in the city of New Orleans, deaths caused by the same murderer who stole the life of the beautiful ghost haunting her dreams night after night.

At first, Jake is afraid that returning home has simply awakened some of the fear of the past...

But as Ashley's nightmares continue, a body count begins to accrue in the city...

And it's suddenly a race to stop a killer before Hallow's Eve comes to a crashing end, with dozens more lives at stake, not to mention heart, soul, and life for Jake and Ashley themselves.

* * * *

Crimson Twilight: A Krewe of Hunters Novella

It's a happy time for Sloan Trent and Jane Everett. What could be happier than the event of their wedding? Their Krewe friends will all be there and the event will take place in a medieval castle transported brick by brick to the New England coast. Everyone is festive and thrilled... until the priest turns up dead just hours before the nuptials. Jane and Sloan must find the truth behind the man and the murder--the secrets of the living and the dead--before they find themselves bound for eternity-- not in wedded bliss but in the darkness of an historical wrong and their own brutal deaths.

* * * *

When Irish Eyes Are Haunting: A Krewe of Hunters Novella

Devin Lyle and Craig Rockwell are back, this time to a haunted castle in Ireland where a banshee may have gone wild—or maybe there's a much more rational explanation—one that involves a disgruntled heir, murder, and mayhem, all with that sexy light touch Heather Graham has turned into her trademark style.

* * * *

All Hallows Eve: A Krewe of Hunters Novella

Salem was a place near and dear to Jenny Duffy and Samuel Hall -- it was where they'd met on a strange and sinister case. They never dreamed that they'd be called back. That history could repeat itself in a most macabre and terrifying fashion. But, then again, it was Salem at Halloween. Seasoned Krewe members, they still find themselves facing the unspeakable horrors in a desperate race to save each other-and perhaps even their very souls.

* * * *

Blood on the Bayou: A Cafferty & Quinn Novella

It's winter and a chill has settled over the area near New Orleans, finding a stream of blood, a tourist follows it to a dead man, face down in the bayou.

The man has been done in by a vicious beating, so violent that his skull has been crushed in.

It's barely a day before a second victim is found... once again so badly thrashed that the water runs red. The city becomes riddled with fear.

An old family friend comes to Danni Cafferty, telling her that he's terrified, he's certain that he's received a message from the Blood Bayou killer--It's your turn to pay, blood on the bayou.

Cafferty and Quinn quickly become involved, and--as they all begin to realize that a gruesome local history is being repeated--they find themselves in a fight to save not just a friend, but, perhaps, their very own lives.

Haunted House
A Krewe of Hunters Novella
By Heather Graham

Halloween! Strange things are going to happen and every year, while loving the holiday, members of the Krewe of Hunters also dread it.

Something somewhere is bound to happen.

And it does.

Krewe member Jon Dickson's fiancée Kylie Connelly is contacted by an old friend who has just moved to Salem, Massachusetts, when the unimaginable happens as the holiday approaches.

Jenny Auger has just managed to buy the historic home of her dreams. But it comes with far more history than she ever imagined—the skeletal remains of seven victims interred in the old walls of the house years and years before—along with a threatening curse.

And strange things are happening in the city. Bizarre attacks...murders that mimic days of old.

With Halloween on the way.

Kylie has a history with the city of Salem, and her strange talent for being within the minds of those under attack—first realized in the city—remains sharp.

But the situation is far more dire than what they have discovered, with strange events and attacks occurring.

And with all their talent for crime solving—with help from the living and the dead—it still remains to be seen if they can solve the murders of the past before Halloween, and the bloodbath that just might occur if the sins of a time gone by cannot be brought to light.

* * * *

Chapter 1

The thing seemed to stare at her.

Of course, it couldn't stare. There was nothing but stygian emptiness where the eyes should have been. The soft tissue had long ago decomposed. And still...

She knew she was in Salem, Massachusetts, renowned for tragic history and ghost stories. And it was almost Halloween. October. *Haunted Happenings* was coming into full swing, filled with scary fun and delight and...

This.

Dear Lord, it was something straight out of a horror movie. Except that...

It was real!

She was dreaming. Somehow, Kylie Connelly Dickson knew she was dreaming. She also knew that, somehow, the dream was real.

And she knew where she was and what was going on—as if she had entered the very soul of another human being.

She was in an old house. One known for its tragic history, curses, hauntings, and all that came with such a place.

Once, Kylie hadn't understood. Now, since she'd met Jon, she knew something about her unique talent—enough to know that she was seeing, feeling, and *knowing* things as another person.

And she knew the circumstances because she had the memories and information of the soul she had entered.

She *was* another person at the moment.

She even knew who she was this time...her friend, Brenda Riley.

And she knew that she had just purchased the home. She knew what Brenda did because, in a very strange way, she *was* Brenda. She saw with her eyes, felt her emotions. Knew her thoughts.

Which told her that the electricity wouldn't be on until later. Unfortunately, the realtor handling the sale hadn't thought she'd be able to get into the home until tomorrow. But, as it turned out, she had signed the last papers today.

It had been a lifelong dream to buy the amazingly historic home in the city she loved so very much. Mandy Nichols, the realtor for the absentee seller, had been wonderful, hurrying things along as best she could, knowing how much Brenda loved the house.

But this...

She was amazed that she hadn't screamed. Maybe because—in the Halloween season—all kinds of pranks and shenanigans went on. Or perhaps, more likely, it was because all her breath was gone, and she had nearly passed out. And though her flashlight reflected off the white gleam of the skull and other skeletal remains stuffed behind the deteriorating false wall, she still hadn't moved.

Because she was frozen stiff with shock and fear.

The house that had stood before had belonged to a woman accused of witchcraft. Not one who had been executed, but one who had died, nonetheless. Her family had left Salem, cursing the very ground. Sometime after their marriage, it was said that Ezekiel Johnson murdered his wife. And in the 1800s, Priscilla Alcott had, in turn, murdered her husband. And then, in the 1900s, Fisher Smith had been accused by the locals of being a serial killer after citizens of Salem, Peabody, and other nearby towns disappeared. Even in 2001, a ghost tour guide had vanished after pointing out the house, the ghosts of the dead who haunted it, and stating how the land itself had been cursed.

But this…

It had to be a prank.

A prank, a prank, a prank…

But it wasn't.

About Heather Graham

New York Times and *USA Today* bestselling author, Heather Graham, majored in theater arts at the University of South Florida. After a stint of several years in dinner theater, back-up vocals, and bartending, she stayed home after the birth of her third child and began to write. Her first book was with Dell, and since then, she has written over two hundred novels and novellas including category, suspense, historical romance, vampire fiction, time travel, occult and Christmas family fare.

She is pleased to have been published in approximately twenty-five languages. She has written over 200 novels and has 60 million books in print. She has been honored with awards from booksellers and writers' organizations for excellence in her work, and she is also proud to be a recipient of the Silver Bullet Award from the International Thriller Writers and was also awarded the prestigious Thriller Master in 2016. She is also a recipient of the Lifetime Achievement Award from RWA. Heather has had books selected for the Doubleday Book Club and the Literary Guild, and has been quoted, interviewed, or featured in such publications as The Nation, Redbook, Mystery Book Club, People and USA Today and appeared on many newscasts including Today, Entertainment Tonight and local television.

Heather loves travel and anything that has to do with the water and is a certified scuba diver. She also loves ballroom dancing. Each year she hosts a ball or dinner theater raising money for the Pediatric Aids Society and in 2006 she hosted the first Writers for New Orleans Workshop to benefit the stricken Gulf Region. She is also the founder of "The Slush Pile Players," presenting something that's "almost like entertainment" for various conferences and benefits. Married since high school graduation and the mother of five, her greatest love in life remains her family, but she also believes her career has been an incredible gift, and she is grateful every day to be doing something that she loves so very much for a living.

Discover 1001 Dark Nights

ABANDON by Rachel Van Dyken ~ THE OPEN DOOR by Laurelin Paige~ CLOSER by Kylie Scott ~ SOMETHING JUST LIKE THIS by Jennifer Probst ~ BLOOD NIGHT by Heather Graham ~ TWIST OF FATE by Jill Shalvis ~ MORE THAN PLEASURE YOU by Shayla Black ~ WONDER WITH ME by Kristen Proby ~ THE DARKEST ASSASSIN by Gena Showalter

COLLECTION EIGHT
DRAGON REVEALED by Donna Grant ~ CAPTURED IN INK by Carrie Ann Ryan ~ SECURING JANE by Susan Stoker ~ WILD WIND by Kristen Ashley ~ DARE TO TEASE by Carly Phillips ~ VAMPIRE by Rebecca Zanetti ~ MAFIA KING by Rachel Van Dyken ~ THE GRAVEDIGGER'S SON by Darynda Jones ~ FINALE by Skye Warren ~ MEMORIES OF YOU by J. Kenner ~ SLAYED BY DARKNESS by Alexandra Ivy ~ TREASURED by Lexi Blake ~ THE DAREDEVIL by Dylan Allen ~ BOND OF DESTINY by Larissa Ione ~ MORE THAN POSSESS YOU by Shayla Black ~ HAUNTED HOUSE by Heather Graham ~ MAN FOR ME by Laurelin Paige ~ THE RHYTHM METHOD by Kylie Scott ~ JONAH BENNETT by Tijan ~ CHANGE WITH ME by Kristen Proby ~ THE DARKEST DESTINY by Gena Showalter

Discover Blue Box Press
TAME ME by J. Kenner ~ TEMPT ME by J. Kenner ~ DAMIEN by J. Kenner ~ TEASE ME by J. Kenner ~ REAPER by Larissa Ione ~ THE SURRENDER GATE by Christopher Rice ~ SERVICING THE TARGET by Cherise Sinclair ~ THE LAKE OF LEARNING by Steve Berry and M.J. Rose ~ THE MUSEUM OF MYSTERIES by Steve Berry and M.J. Rose ~ TEASE ME by J. Kenner ~ FROM BLOOD AND ASH by Jennifer L. Armentrout ~ QUEEN MOVE by Kennedy Ryan ~ THE HOUSE OF LONG AGO by Steve Berry and M.J. Rose ~ THE BUTTERFLY ROOM by Lucinda Riley ~ A KINGDOM OF FLESH AND FIRE by Jennifer L. Armentrout ~ THE LAST TIARA by M.J. Rose ~ THE CROWN OF GILDED BONES by Jennifer L. Armentrout ~ THE MISSING SISTER by Lucinda Riley ~ THE END OF FOREVER by Steve Berry and M.J. Rose ~ THE STEAL by C. W. Gortner and M.J. Rose ~ CHASING SERENITY by Kristen Ashley ~ A SHADOW IN THE EMBER by Jennifer L. Armentrout

On Behalf of 1001 Dark Nights,

Liz Berry, M.J. Rose, and Jillian Stein would like to thank ~

Steve Berry
Doug Scofield
Benjamin Stein
Kim Guidroz
Social Butterfly PR
Asha Hossain
Chris Graham
Chelle Olson
Kasi Alexander
Jessica Saunders
Dylan Stockton
Kate Boggs
Richard Blake
and Simon Lipskar

Made in the USA
Columbia, SC
13 October 2024